Life
Between the Lines

Life
Between the Lines

Sameer Sagar

The Thoughtivation

Copyright © Sameer Sagar 2025
All rights reserved.

For my late sister

Khushbu

CONTENTS

ACKNOWLEDGMENTS

First and foremost, I express my heartfelt gratitude to Lord Krishna for His divine blessings and guidance throughout this journey.

To my parents, thank you for being the foundation of my personality and the constant source of my values and strength.

To my wife, Juhi, your unwavering trust in me and your encouragement to embark on this project have been my greatest motivation. This book would not have been possible without your support and belief in my vision.

A special thanks to my best friends, Ashwin, Prathamesh, and Atishay Jain, whose honest and brutal guidance has shaped my journey and pushed me to improve at every step.

There is no Mr. Soni without the support of you sweet people—each of you has contributed to the spirit of this book.

Lastly, to all my students, you are the essence of my teaching journey. Each of you holds a small but significant part of my conscience, and this book is a reflection of all those lessons we have shared together.

1

WHAT GOES AROUND

The sun painted the morning sky in soft shades of gold as Mr. Soni walked briskly to school. It was the first day of the new academic year, a day he always looked forward to with childlike enthusiasm. The crispness of freshly cleaned classrooms, the laughter of old students reconnecting, and the promise of new faces joining—it was all a recipe for excitement.

When he stepped into his assigned classroom, however, the lively picture in his mind shattered immediately.

The classroom was in chaos. Desks were skewed at odd angles, books lay abandoned on the floor, and the air was thick with tension. In the center of the room, Parv and Rajveer, two of his students, were grappling with each other. Their faces were flushed with anger as they pushed and shouted, oblivious to the onlookers around them.

The other students stood frozen, their expressions a mix of shock and discomfort. No one intervened; they were mere spectators, unsure of how to react.

Mr. Soni raised his voice, firm and commanding. "Stop this madness right now!"

The classroom fell silent as the boys froze mid-motion. Parv's hand was still clutching Rajveer's collar, and Rajveer's fist was raised in retaliation. Slowly, they separated, their breaths coming in quick bursts, their eyes still locked in animosity.

"Both of you, to the front," Mr. Soni ordered, his tone leaving no room for argument. Parv and Rajveer shuffled to the front of the class, their heads hanging low.

"Class, take your seats," Mr. Soni said, addressing the onlookers. The students quickly returned to their desks, the earlier noise replaced by a tense quiet.

Mr. Soni stood between the two boys, his arms crossed. "What happened here?"

"He started it!" Parv said, pointing at Rajveer.

"That's not true!" Rajveer shot back. "You called me a cheat in front of everyone!"

The room filled with murmurs as the students tried to piece together the argument. Mr. Soni held up his hand, silencing them.

"Enough," he said firmly. "I don't care who started it. What I care about is that this behavior is unacceptable."

He picked up a piece of chalk and drew a small circle on the blackboard. "Do you know what this is?"

The class stared at the circle, confused.

"This," he said, "is a chain reaction. It represents how our actions ripple through the world."

Mr. Soni turned back to the class. "Settle down, everyone," he said gently. "Let me tell you a story. Probably it's the first time I'm telling a story when I am angry, settle down and listen carefully because I want this incident to become a history. The one that is not going to repeat itself, Ever…"

Mr. Soni looked outside the window, took his familiar comfortable stance at the desk and promptly jumped into the story.

****

Years ago, in Mumbai there used to live Motiram, he was a 60-year-old accountant, and had worked at an accounting firm, Seth Hakumchand & Co., for the past 40 years.

The small, dimly lit office had been a second home to him, a space where dusty ledgers and ink-stained fingers were part of his life's rhythm. For Seth Hakumchand, his boss, Motiram was not just an employee but the invisible pillar who kept the accounts running smoothly.

That day, however, the air in the office was different. Seth Hakumchand, known for his stern but fair demeanor, sat slouched at his large teakwood desk. Lines of frustration etched deeper into his already aging face.

Some personal issue — maybe a family squabble or a bad investment, perhaps — had been gnawing at him since morning. The staff knew better than to cross his path on days like these.

Motiram, unaware, shuffled to Seth's table at lunchtime to hand over some updated ledgers. His old, thin shoulders slightly stooped, his hands clutching the books carefully, like they were priceless artifacts.

"Can't you do anything right?" Seth bellowed suddenly, his voice echoing through the silent office. Motiram froze. "What's the point of keeping you around, Motiram, if you can't even handle a simple task?" Seth hurled the papers aside, the sheets fluttering to the ground like wounded birds. Without any explanation Seth Hakumchand stormed out of the office. "Useless…"

Motiram stood there, flabbergasted, his heart sinking. The words pierced him deeper than he let on.

For a man who prided himself on his precision and loyalty, this unprovoked anger felt like betrayal. Without a word, he quietly picked up the scattered sheets, his hands trembling. His colleagues watched from a distance, pretending to work but unable to look away.

That day, Motiram did something he hadn't done in years — he left early. As he walked home through the crowded Mumbai streets, the usual sounds of life — the clanging of rickshaws, vendors shouting their wares — blurred around him. A tight knot sat in his chest, heavy and suffocating.

At home, the stillness felt suffocating too. His son, Sohan, greeted him at the door. Sohan, in his mid-thirties, worked at a private firm, always rushing between deadlines. Seeing his father home early, he paused. "Baba, you're back so soon. Is everything okay?"

The question snapped something inside Motiram. "What do you care?" he barked, his voice louder than it had been in years.

Sohan recoiled, his brows furrowing in surprise. "Do you think you understand my life, Sohan? Do you?"

Without waiting for a response, Motiram stomped into his room, shutting the door behind him. The sound echoed like a slap.

Sohan stood in the hallway, the sting of his father's anger still hanging in the air. He wasn't used to seeing Baba like this — so brittle, so unlike himself. Frustration churned in his chest, an unformed resentment seeking an outlet. It's not in Indian Sanskaar to talk back to father.

"Claaaang…" a sound of some utensils falling and scattering reverberated through the whole house.

He turned sharply towards the kitchen, where Neha, his wife, was frantically trying to pick up the utensils. She looked up, smiling faintly. "You're back early, too?" she asked.

"Can't you just do something quietly for once, Neha?" Sohan snapped, his voice sharper than intended.

Neha flinched, her hand pausing mid-air.

"What? What did I even do?" she said, hurt flashing across her face. But Sohan was already walking away, muttering under his breath.

The anger passed to Neha like a baton in a relay race. She had to silence her anger, after all "How could a Bechaari wife retort to her Patidev?" She stood there for a moment, blinking back tears, before slamming the knife onto the cutting board.

"Vinnie!" she yelled, turning toward the living room.

Vinnie, their teenage daughter, was sprawled on the couch, her feet propped up as the TV blared some cartoon she wasn't really watching. At her mother's shout, she sat up with an exaggerated groan. "What now, Maa?"

"Do something useful for once! You're always sitting here like a princess," Neha shot back.

Vinnie narrowed her eyes, anger bubbling up. "I wasn't even bothering anyone!" she muttered, but her mother was already banging pots in the kitchen.

Vinnie stomped upstairs to her room, her mind a whirlwind of frustration. She shoved the door open to find Jay, her younger brother, sitting on the floor with his harmonica. The gentle, cheerful tune grated on her nerves like nails on a chalkboard.

"Get out of my room, Jay!" she yelled.

Jay, who had slipped into the meditative form producing music, froze mid-note, the harmonica still pressed to his lips. "What's your problem?"

He mumbled, confused.

"Just get the hell out!" Vinnie snapped, pointing to the door. Now that was what I always call an Elder Sibling Behaviour.

Jay glared at her, stuffing the Harmonica into his pocket. Without another word, he stomped out of the house, his small fists clenched.

Outside, the late afternoon sun hung low, and the air was thick with the usual chaos of the neighborhood.

Jay walked aimlessly until he reached Nana-Nani Park. His sneakers crunched over the gravel path as he muttered angrily to himself.

Spotting a stray dog sniffing at a pile of leaves near a bench, Jay's frustration found its target.

He kicked the dog tightly on its rump.

The poor dog yelped, its bark sharp and echoing in the empty park. It bolted, disappearing into the bushes. Jay felt a twinge of guilt, but his anger lingered as he slumped onto a bench.

That evening, as the sky turned a murky gray, Seth Hakumchand, unaware of the whirlwind he had created in so many lives, still fuming since the morning, decided to clear his mind with a walk. Nana-Nani Park was his usual spot — a brief respite from the chaos of the world.

The park was quiet, except for the rustle of leaves and the occasional distant bark. Seth didn't notice the dog lurking near the path until it lunged. The bite was sudden, sharp, and searing with pain. Seth cried out, collapsing to the ground as the stray barked and vanished into the shadows.

The next morning, Motiram arrived at Seth Hakumchand & Co. only to find the office locked. A notice on the door read:
"Office closed for 4 days. Seth Hukamchand on bed rest."

Confused, Motiram asked around and learned of Seth's accident. Something stirred within him — an old loyalty, perhaps. That afternoon, Motiram purchased a small bouquet of marigolds and a Get Well Soon card.

At Seth's house, the air smelled of antiseptics and regret. Seth, propped up on pillows, looked pale and subdued. When he saw Motiram enter, he managed a small smile.

"Oh Motiram, my friend, come." Seth said softly, his voice no longer sharp. "I have something to tell you, I wronged you yesterday, and I have received the fruit of my wrong deed. I'm sorry. I had no reason to speak to you like that."

Motiram, holding the flowers awkwardly, said nothing but nodded slowly.

Seth continued slowly, "When the office reopens, I want you to head the accounts department. You've earned it."

Motiram placed the flowers beside Seth's bed. For the first time in days, the knot in his chest loosened.

Outside,
Life continued its endless ripple. Somewhere in Nana-Nani Park, a stray dog slept under a tree, unaware that its bite had set everything back into balance.

****

As Mr. Soni finished the story, the classroom remained silent, the weight of his words settling over the students.

He turned back to Parv and Rajveer. "So, such was the story of Karma. Fun apart, the story teaches us something. Let's talk about what just happened here. Parv, why did you call Rajveer a cheat?"

Parv shuffled his feet, looking uncomfortable. "He won the math quiz yesterday, sir. I — I thought he might have copied my answers. I wasn't sure, But..."

Mr. Soni raised an eyebrow. "So, you assumed without proof and accused him publicly?"

Parv nodded, his head hanging low.

"And Rajveer," Mr. Soni said, turning to him, "how did you respond?"

"I got angry, sir," Rajveer admitted, his voice barely above a whisper. "I did cheat a little, to be honest, but I felt humiliated by Parv's public confrontation. So, I lost my temper."

"Do you see how both of you contributed to this fight?" Mr. Soni asked, his gaze shifting between them. "Parv, your words sowed anger in Rajveer's mind. When you could've called him aside and talked to him in a peaceful manner. While Rajveer, your reaction escalated the situation. And look where it led—not just to a fight, but to a classroom full of students who felt uneasy and upset."

The two boys looked at each other, guilt flickering in their eyes.

Mr. Soni turned back to the chalkboard and drew a larger circle around the first. "But here's the good news," he said. "This circle doesn't have to carry negativity. Just as anger spreads, so does kindness."

He faced the class, his voice steady. "Think about it. If you had chosen kindness instead of anger, what would have happened? Parv, what if you had spoken to Rajveer privately and asked him about the quiz instead of accusing him?"

Parv hesitated, then said, "Maybe…maybe we could have talked it out."

"Exactly," Mr. Soni said with a nod. "And Rajveer, what if you had responded calmly, explaining your side without anger?"

Rajveer frowned in thought. "I guess it wouldn't have turned into a fight. I think Parv would have agreed to help me out understanding the lessons as well."

"Right," Mr. Soni said. "Kindness and understanding can

stop a negative chain reaction before it even begins. And when you choose kindness, it doesn't just affect you. It spreads, creating a ripple of positivity that touches everyone around you."

He paused, letting his words sink in. Then he turned to the rest of the class. "You were all witnesses to what happened. How many of you felt uncomfortable or upset seeing your classmates fight?"

Several hands went up, and a murmur of agreement rippled through the room.

"You see?" Mr. Soni said. "Your actions don't exist in a vacuum. They affect everyone. That's why it's so important to think before you act or speak."

He turned back to Parv and Rajveer. "Now, I want both of you to start a new chain reaction — one of kindness. Parv, what do you want to say to Rajveer?"

Parv took a deep breath. "I'm sorry, Rajveer. I shouldn't have called you a cheat."

Rajveer hesitated, then nodded. "I'm sorry too. I shouldn't have reacted the way I did."

Mr. Soni smiled, a small but genuine expression. "Good. That's a start. Now, I want you both to remember this lesson: what you put into the world comes back to you. If you choose kindness, it will create a ripple that makes everyone's lives better, including your own."

The tension in the room began to lift, replaced by a sense of unity. The students sat a little straighter, whispered a little softer, and looked at each other with a little more understanding.

As Mr. Soni moved on to the day's lesson, he felt a quiet satisfaction. The classroom wasn't perfect, but it was on its way to becoming a space of kindness and harmony.

<h1 style="text-align:center">2</h1>

I GOT YOUR BACK

The school auditorium buzzed with excitement as the Guru Poornima celebrations were in full swing. The hall was adorned with garlands and colorful banners that read, "Honoring Our Gurus." Students were seated in neat rows, eagerly waiting for their turn to perform. Teachers sat proudly in the front row, their faces reflecting both pride and anticipation.

Daksh, the confident young anchor, stepped onto the stage, holding the microphone like a seasoned professional. "Ladies and gentlemen, Guru Poornima is not just a celebration, but a moment to honor those who have shaped our lives. We've had wonderful speeches, melodious songs, and heartfelt shlokas so far. Now, let's hear from one of the most beloved teachers of our school, Mr. Soni!"

The applause from the students was deafening, as all eyes turned toward Mr. Soni, seated in the corner of the teacher's section. Dressed in his usual neat kurta, he smiled warmly but shook his head gently.

"No, no, Daksh," Mr. Soni said humbly, "Let the seniors share their wisdom today. I am merely a storyteller for my students."

Before Daksh could reply, Ms. Pathak, a senior teacher known for her sharp tongue and sense of humor, leaned back in her chair and spoke loudly enough for everyone to hear.

"Oh, why would he say anything to all of you? All his grand stories are for his precious students only!"

Laughter rippled through the crowd, but a hush fell over the students who loved Mr. Soni dearly. They noticed the flicker of hurt in his eyes, though he quickly masked it with a soft smile.

Daksh, flustered, tried to change the subject, but Mr. Soni stood up. "It's all right, Daksh," he said calmly, adjusting his glasses. "If Ms. Pathak feels that way, perhaps I should share something with everyone today. After all, stories aren't just for students; they are for anyone willing to listen and learn."

The students erupted into applause, cheering for their favorite teacher. Even the other teachers sat up straight, intrigued by what he might say.

As Mr. Soni walked up to the stage, his calm demeanor and steady steps silenced the entire hall. The room felt lighter, as if everyone knew they were about to hear something profound.

He adjusted the microphone, his voice steady and rich as he began, "Today is a day to honor our Gurus, our guides, our teachers. It reminds me of a story...a story of devotion, courage, and the sacred bond between a Guru and his disciple. Let me tell you the story of Chhatrapati Shivaji Maharaj and his revered Guru, Samarth Ramdas Swami."

****

Chhatrapati Shivaji Maharaj was a very faithful devotee of his Guru, Samarth Ramdas Swami. Samarth used to love him more than any other of his disciples. Seeing this, the other disciples of Samarth started to feel that since Shivaji Maharaj is a king, he is the Guru's favourite. Samarth decided to remove this misunderstanding of his disciples. So, he once took all his disciples to the forest.

It was a bright morning when Samarth Ramdas Swami, the wise and beloved Guru, decided to take his disciples on a walk through the dense forest near their village. The birds chirped melodiously, and the air was filled with the sweet scent of blooming flowers. But as the group ventured deeper into the forest, the mood began to shift. The disciples looked around nervously; the trees seemed taller, and the paths grew narrower.

"Stay close," Samarth said with a calm smile. "This forest has its secrets."

As the sun began to dip below the horizon, the disciples realized they had lost their way. The forest seemed endless, and the once-lively chatter faded into uneasy silence.

Samarth led them to a small cave nestled between two large rocks. Once inside, he sat down, closed his eyes for a moment, and then suddenly clutched his stomach, groaning in pain.

"Gurudev!" cried Gopal, the youngest disciple. "What's wrong?"

Samarth winced and lay down on the rocky floor. "It's my abdomen…a terrible pain has struck me."

The disciples gathered around him, their faces pale with worry. "What can we do to help, Gurudev?" Hari asked, his voice trembling.

Samarth opened his eyes slightly. "There is only one

remedy for this illness," he said in a weak voice. "But it is nearly impossible to obtain."

"What is it, Gurudev?" asked Gopal desperately.

"The fresh milk of a tigress," Samarth replied. "But don't trouble yourselves. It's too dangerous."

The disciples exchanged uneasy glances. "A tigress? In this forest?" Gopal whispered, fear evident in his voice. None of them dared to speak further.

Meanwhile, far away in his grand fort, Chhatrapati Shivaji Maharaj, the brave king and devoted disciple of Samarth, had just returned from a meeting. Upon hearing that his Guru had gone into the forest, he grew concerned. "Gurudev is in the forest with his disciples? I must check on him," Shivaji thought, and without hesitation, he set off without waiting for any helper to accompany him.

As Shivaji wandered through the forest, he heard a faint groaning sound. His sharp instincts guided him toward the cave. When he entered, he saw Samarth lying on the ground, surrounded by his anxious disciples.

"Gurudev! What has happened?" Shivaji asked, kneeling by his side.

Samarth looked up and said softly, "I am in great pain, Shivaba. The only cure is fresh tigress milk. But it is too dangerous."

Without a moment's hesitation, Shivaji stood up. "Don't worry, Gurudev. I will bring the milk."

The disciples watched in awe as Shivaji bowed before Samarth and left the cave, determination shining in his eyes.

Shivaji wandered deeper into the forest, his senses alert. Soon, he spotted two tiger cubs playing near a bush. He paused, knowing their mother couldn't be far. Sure enough, a tigress emerged, her piercing eyes fixed on him. She let out a low growl, her body tensed to protect her cubs.

All the instincts in his mind told him to pull out the Sword from its scabbard hanging from his cummerbund and defend himself against the ferocious beast. But he knew that this was not the time for fighting, His teacher needed this remedy. So he decided to try something uncharacteristic. He unbuckled the sword with one hand and placed it gently on the floor as the gesture of meekness.

Shivaji, unarmed and calm, folded his hands in respect. "O Mother of the Forest," he said gently, "I have not come to harm you or your little ones. I need your milk to save my Guru's life. Please help me, and I promise in return I will not harm you or the cubs."

The tigress growled again, but Shivaji's calm voice and respectful demeanor seemed to soothe her. Slowly, he knelt down, extending his hand. "You are a mother, and you understand the pain of seeing a loved one suffer. Please allow me to help my Guru."

To his unspoken amazement, the tigress stopped growling. She sat down, her sharp eyes softening. Shivaji carefully approached her, gently patted her back, and milked her into the pot he had brought.

"Thank you, Mother," he said, bowing deeply. With the pot in hand, he hurried back to the cave.

When Shivaji returned, the disciples were stunned. They couldn't believe their eyes as he handed the pot of tigress milk to Samarth.

"Here, Gurudev," Shivaji said, bowing. "I have brought what you need."

Samarth smiled warmly and placed his hand on Shivaji's head. "You have proven once again, Shivaba, that devotion and courage can overcome any obstacle."

Turning to the other disciples, Samarth said, "Do you now understand why Shivaji is dear to me? It is not because he is a king but because he is selfless, fearless, and devoted. While you hesitated, he acted. While you feared for your safety, he risked his life for me."

The disciples lowered their heads in shame. "Forgive us, Gurudev," Gopal said. "We were blinded by jealousy and failed to see the depth of Maharaj's devotion."

Samarth nodded. "Jealousy weakens the spirit and clouds judgment. Instead of envying others, learn from their virtues. If you want to earn my love and respect, work on your own weaknesses and strive to become better disciples."

Samarth turned back to Shivaji. "You have shown us all the power of true devotion. May your courage and love inspire these disciples and countless others."

Shivaji bowed deeply. "Gurudev, your blessings are my greatest strength."

The disciples left the forest with a renewed sense of purpose, carrying the powerful lesson in their hearts. Now they realised that if a Guru loves a particular disciple, it is because he is worthy of it. He is worthy of that special grace. Jealousy increases one's weakness and defects. So, instead of being jealous of such a worthy disciple we should try to remove our weaknesses and defects. The story of Shivaji Maharaj and the tigress would be passed down through generations, teaching children and adults alike about the virtues of courage, devotion, and selflessness.

******

When Mr. Soni concluded the story, there was a profound silence in the room.

"You see, children, such was the unwavering faith Swami Samarth had in the bravery and obedience of Chhatrapati Shivaji Maharaj. But even more than that, today, the people of Maharashtra remember him for his powerful words: 'Bhiu Nakos, Mi Tujhya Pathishi Aahe,' which translates to, 'Don't be afraid, I have got your back.'

And today, I want to share that same message with all of you—whatever challenges life may throw your way, no matter how difficult the road ahead seems, remember this: never be afraid. Just like Shivaji had his Guru's support, you too have someone by your side. I have got your back."

A wave of applause erupted, louder and more heartfelt than any before it. Students clapped enthusiastically, and even the teachers joined in with admiration.

Mr. Soni stepped back from the microphone, giving a modest bow before speaking one last time. "You see, my dear students, stories are not just about entertainment. They carry lessons that guide us, inspire us, and show us the power of devotion, humility, and courage. Whether we are teachers or students, young or old, these lessons are for everyone. And that is the bond we celebrate on Guru Poornima."

As Mr. Soni returned to his seat, Ms. Pathak stood up and approached him. "Mr. Soni," she said softly, "that was…beautiful. I shouldn't have teased you earlier. You truly have a gift for teaching, one that extends far beyond the classroom."

Mr. Soni smiled warmly. "Thank you, Ms. Pathak. It's never about who we teach, but how we share the lessons. Stories have a way of reaching everyone."

The event ended on a high note, with the story of Shivaji and Samarth Ramdas Swami etched into the hearts of everyone present, a testament to the power of respect, devotion, and the timeless wisdom of storytelling.

3
DREAM BIG

The morning sun streamed through the classroom windows as a cool breeze whispered through the slightly ajar shutters. It was a relaxed Saturday, the kind where even the usually stern ringing of the school bell seemed less commanding. The students of Class 10 sat in their seats, chatting and passing notes, still adjusting to the rhythm of the new academic year.

In the midst of this lighthearted atmosphere, Mr. Soni walked into the classroom. Dressed in his usual crisp white shirt and trousers, he carried a small stack of papers in one hand and a serene smile on his face. He set the papers down on his desk, turned to face the students, and clapped his hands once to grab their attention.

"Alright, settle down, everyone," he said, his calm voice cutting through the chatter. "I know it's a Saturday, and I won't burden you with heavy lessons today. But I do want to discuss something important."

The students exchanged curious glances as Mr. Soni continued. "Tell me—what is your target in life? What do you want to become?"

For a moment, there was silence, punctuated only by the

rustling of leaves outside the window. Then, a few hands hesitantly went up.

"I haven't decided yet, sir," said one boy from the back.

"Me neither," added another.

"I'll probably take over my father's shop," said Aniket, a boy sitting in the middle row.

"Government job for me," said Priya confidently.

Mr. Soni nodded thoughtfully. "Alright. What about the rest of you? Surely someone here has a big dream?"

A girl named Neha raised her hand. "I want to become an IAS officer, sir," she said, her voice steady.

"Good, Neha! A clear and ambitious goal," Mr. Soni said with an encouraging nod.

Then, as the murmur of agreement spread through the class, Rajveer, the class clown, shot up from his seat with a mischievous grin. "Sir, I've decided! I'm going to become Elon Musk—the richest man on Earth!"

The classroom erupted in laughter. A few students whistled; others banged their desks in mock applause. "Elon Musk!" someone exclaimed between fits of laughter. "Good luck, Rajveer!"

Rajveer, basking in the attention, gave an exaggerated bow.

But Mr. Soni raised his hand, the universal signal for silence. Slowly, the laughter died down, and the students turned their attention back to him.

"It's okay to dream big," Mr. Soni began, his voice calm but firm. "In fact, it's necessary. Without a dream, you have no direction. And yes, Rajveer, even your dream of becoming Elon Musk is valid. Do you know why?"

Rajveer blinked, his grin fading slightly. "Why, sir?"

"Because dreams, no matter how big, serve as a map for your life. They tell you what you need to do, how much effort you need to put in. The bigger the dream, the greater the need for hard work."

He walked to the blackboard and picked up a piece of chalk. Drawing a quick sketch of a well, he turned back to face the class. "To bring water from a well, you must dig at least 50 feet into the ground. You cannot dig five feet here, then five feet there, and expect to find water, can you?"

The students were silent, pondering his words.

"But sir," one of the boys finally spoke up, "isn't it better to be realistic? What's the point of dreaming about something that's impossible?"

Mr. Soni smiled, leaning against his desk. "Realistic dreams, you say? Alright. Let me tell you a story. It's about two friends, Jay and Raju. And perhaps, by the end of it, you'll understand why dreaming big matters."

****

The sun hung low over Rampur, casting a golden glow on the sprawling fields. The air was thick with the earthy scent of freshly tilled soil, and the rhythmic sound of bullock carts in the distance punctuated the calm. Jay and Raju, two boys on the cusp of adulthood, sat under the shade of a neem tree, their backs resting against its rough bark.

Jay looked up at the sky, squinting at the clouds. "Raju, do you ever feel like you're meant for something more?"

Raju plucked a blade of grass, twirling it between his fingers. "More than what? The fields, the cows, or the endless debts our families can barely repay?"

Jay's voice brimmed with excitement. "Exactly! Look at us—stuck in this cycle of planting and harvesting, living the same lives our fathers and grandfathers did. I want to break free, Raju. I want to see the world, own it even!"

Raju laughed, his tone playful but skeptical. "Own the world? Jay, we can't even afford to fix the leaking roof over our heads."

Jay ignored him, his imagination ablaze. "You'll see. One day, I'll be rich. I'll have a plane, a palace, industries that stretch across the city. And my wife—she'll be the most beautiful woman anyone's ever seen, a famous actress perhaps."

Raju snorted, shaking his head. "An actress? And how do you plan to get all this? Do you have some secret treasure hidden away that I don't know about?"

Jay grinned, undeterred. "No treasure. Just dreams. Big dreams. And hard work."

Raju leaned back, resting his hands on the ground. "Big dreams, huh? Well, good luck with that. My dream's much simpler. I'll save up enough to buy a small house and a little farm. I'll marry Radha—she's sweet, simple, and kind. We'll have a couple of kids, and I'll spend my life in peace. No planes, no palaces. Just a happy, quiet life."

Jay turned to him, his expression incredulous. "That's it? That's your dream?"

Raju smiled. "Yes, and it's enough for me."

Jay laughed, shaking his head. "You, my friend, have a loser's dream. You're thinking too small! If you don't dream big, how will you ever achieve anything great?"

"And you," Raju shot back, "have what I'd call a pachyderm dream. It's so big, it'll crush you under its weight. Be realistic, Jay. You're setting yourself up for disappointment."

The two sat in silence for a moment, the sound of birds returning to their nests filling the air. Jay finally broke the quiet.

"Let's make a pact," he said, his voice firm.

Raju raised an eyebrow. "A pact?"

"Yes. Fifteen years from now, let's meet back here, in Rampur. We'll see who's closer to their dream."

Raju chuckled. "Fine. But don't cry when I remind you of your pachyderm dream."

Jay smirked. "And don't be jealous when I fly in on my plane."

The two friends shook hands, the neem tree standing witness to their promise. As the sun dipped below the horizon, casting the fields in shadow, their laughter echoed across the village, carrying with it the hope and innocence of youth.

Fifteen years had passed since that day under the neem tree. Rampur had changed. The once-sleepy village was now a bustling town, with shops lining the main road and new buildings sprouting where open fields used to be. The scent of wet soil and the sound of chirping crickets still lingered, but the quiet charm of the village had given way to the hum of modernity.

Raju stood outside his modest house, wiping the dust off his old double-decker scooter. It was an early morning ritual, just like dropping his children to school. His 10-year-old daughter, Meera, stood impatiently by the gate, her school bag slung over one shoulder. Beside her, her younger brother, Aryan, mimicked the sound of an engine, giggling as he pretended to drive an invisible car.

"Hurry up, Papa! We'll be late," Meera said, tapping her foot.

"Patience, little madam," Raju replied, grinning as he tested the kickstart. "This old fellow needs a bit of coaxing before he's ready to go."

Suddenly, a loud roar filled the air. A shadow passed over them, and Aryan squealed in delight, pointing at the sky.

"Look! A helicopter!"

Raju glanced up, shielding his eyes from the sun. The helicopter was descending, its sleek body gleaming as it hovered over the town center, just across the road from their house. It was rare to see such a thing in Rampur, even with all its recent growth.

"Let's go see it!" Aryan tugged at Raju's arm, his excitement contagious.

"No time for that," Raju said, though his own curiosity was piqued. "You'll miss school."

"But Papa," Meera protested, "it's right there!"

Raju sighed, relenting. "Alright, but only for a minute."

The three of them walked toward the crowd gathering near the town center. The helicopter's blades slowed, the wind kicking up dust as it landed. A man stepped out, dressed in a crisp white shirt and sunglasses, his hair neatly combed.

Raju squinted, a sense of familiarity washing over him. The man scanned the crowd, and his gaze fell on Raju. A smile broke across his face.

"Raju?" he called out, his voice clear and confident.

Raju froze. "Jay?"

Jay walked toward him, arms outstretched. The two friends embraced, their laughter echoing above the murmurs of the crowd.

"It's been so long," Jay said, stepping back to get a better look at Raju. "You haven't changed a bit."

"And you," Raju replied, shaking his head in amazement, "you look… successful."

Jay laughed. "Come, let's catch up properly. Where's your house?"

"Just across the road," Raju said, still processing the moment. "Come, my friend, let me welcome you."

Back at Raju's modest house, Radha served them steaming cups of tea. The children stared wide-eyed at Jay, whispering among themselves.

"Who's this fancy uncle, Papa?" Aryan asked, loud enough for everyone to hear.

Raju chuckled. "This is Jay, my old friend. We grew up together."

"Papa's friend has a helicopter!" Meera whispered to Aryan, as if the machine itself had given Jay some kind of magical status.

Jay smiled at them warmly. "Your father and I used to dream under that neem tree over there," he said, pointing out the window. "And look at him now—he's built a beautiful life."

Radha beamed with pride as Raju tried to deflect the attention. "It's a simple life," he said, handing Jay a plate of freshly fried pakoras. "Now tell me about you. What brings you to Rampur?"

Jay leaned back, sipping his tea. "Oh, I've come here for something special," he said cryptically.

Raju raised an eyebrow. "Special? Come on, don't keep me guessing."

Jay grinned but stayed quiet. "We'll talk about it after lunch."

Lunch was a simple yet hearty meal of dal, rotis, and freshly picked vegetables from Raju's small farm. Jay ate with relish, praising Radha's cooking while Raju couldn't help but notice how effortlessly polished his friend had become.

After the children were sent off to play and Radha busied herself in the kitchen, Raju and Jay sat on the cot in the living room. The room, though modest, exuded warmth—a wall adorned with family photos, a fan creaking overhead, and a faint breeze filtering through the open window.

Raju poured two glasses of buttermilk and handed one to Jay. "So, Jay, we finally meet after all these years. Tell me, my friend—how's life? Remember our pact?"

Jay took a sip, smiling. "Of course, I remember. That neem tree, our big dreams. It feels like yesterday."

Raju leaned forward, a glint of pride in his eyes. "Well, I've fulfilled my dream. I bought this house and the small farm behind it. Radha and I have built a life together. Meera and Aryan—they're my pride and joy. Life's simple, but it's mine."

Jay nodded, his smile genuine. "I'm happy for you, Raju. You've built something meaningful. That's no small feat."

Raju's voice grew teasing. "And you? How about your pachyderm dream? Did you build your palace? Buy that plane? Or are you still chasing the clouds?"

Jay chuckled, shaking his head. "You always had a way with words. No, Raju, I haven't achieved everything I dreamed of."

Raju smirked, leaning back. "I told you, didn't I? Dreaming big is fine, but you should've been realistic. Look at me—I aimed small and hit the target."

Jay's smile faltered for a moment. He set his glass down and looked directly at Raju.

"Do you really think that aiming big is foolish?" he asked, his tone calm but firm.

Raju shrugged. "I just think chasing impossible dreams leads to disappointment. Look at you—you're still not where you wanted to be, are you?"

Jay took a deep breath, his gaze steady. "You're right—I didn't achieve everything I wanted. But let me tell you what I did achieve. I don't have a palace, but I live in a beautiful bungalow in the city. I don't own industries, but I run a thriving cotton mill. And while I don't have a plane, I do have that helicopter parked outside."

Raju blinked, taken aback. "You... own a helicopter?"

Jay nodded. "I do. And that's not all." He reached into his pocket and pulled out a golden envelope, handing it to Raju. "This is the reason I'm here today. It's my wedding invitation."

Raju opened the envelope, his eyes scanning the elegant card. Jay continued, his voice tinged with pride. "I'm marrying a neurosurgeon—a brilliant, compassionate, and, yes, the most beautiful woman I've ever met. Her name is Dr. Asha. She's everything I could've hoped for."

Raju looked up, speechless.

Jay smiled softly. "I didn't come here to boast, Raju. I came because I wanted my childhood friend to share in my happiness. But there's something I've learned over the years, and I want you to know it too."

Raju nodded slowly, still processing Jay's words. "What's that?"

Jay leaned forward, his voice earnest. "Dreams, no matter how big, push us to grow. I didn't achieve everything I set out to, but aiming high brought me further than I ever thought possible. It's not about the end goal—it's about the journey. Teach your children to dream big, Raju. Even if they don't achieve it all, they'll end up with more than they ever imagined."

Raju sat in silence, reflecting. His friend, who he once thought was chasing impossible fantasies, had built a life that was anything but ordinary.

****

"You see, children" said Mr. Soni, "It it necessary to have big dreams in life because they push you beyond the boundaries and they keep motivating you continuously"

"But sir, won't it lead to depression if you couldn't fulfill the impossible dreams?" asked Aniket "I think it is good to have an easy dream and achieve it. It is called practical approach, isn't it?"

"It is practical approach, but dreams don't need to be practical." said Mr. Soni, "Do you think you would be happy living a mediocre life as Raju?"

"But sir isn't it just a story? Anything can happy in a story." Garvit argued "They have also shown in the movies that happiness is necessary. Even a simple hobby like photography can help you acquire more happiness than becoming an engineer."

"Yes, that is correct, But choosing a lesser career or lazing around or having a lower self-esteem is not happiness, is it now? You may have the poverty of money, but you don't need to have poor dreams" Mr. Soni said in his comical way "And besides, Believe it or not but a good career helps you make a good money, and good money can buy you a good amount of happiness. Don't you want to buy you some more happiness when you'd grow old, Garvit?"

The laughter of the students filled up the classroom. Garvit nodded in agreement.

4

CONCENTRATION IS A FRUIT OF OBDURACY

It was a regular Wednesday afternoon, and Mr. Soni's 10th-grade Social Studies class was underway. The warm air drifted lazily through the open windows, and the rhythmic chirping of sparrows filled the otherwise quiet classroom. Mr. Soni, a man known for his sharp observations and calm demeanor, was in the middle of explaining the Indian Freedom Movement when his eyes wandered to the last bench.

Rohit, slumped over his desk, was sound asleep. His head rested awkwardly on his folded arms, and an occasional snore escaped his lips. The class, amused but cautious, stifled their giggles, trying to avoid Mr. Soni's piercing gaze. But Mr. Soni had already noticed.

"Rohit!" Mr. Soni called out, his voice firm but not angry. The boy jolted awake, blinking rapidly as he tried to orient himself.

"Stand up," Mr. Soni said, crossing his arms.

Rohit stood slowly, his eyes still droopy. "Yes, sir?"

"What's the matter? Why were you sleeping in my class?"

The classroom fell silent. Everyone's eyes darted between Mr. Soni and Rohit, anticipating what would happen next.

"Sir... I was just... umm... tired," Rohit mumbled, scratching the back of his head.

"Tired? It's barely noon! What were you doing last night that has left you so exhausted?"

Rohit hesitated, his face turning red. After a moment, he admitted, "Sir, I was up late finishing my math assignments and preparing for today's quiz. I... I didn't realize how late it had gotten."

Before Mr. Soni could respond, Gaurav raised his hand. "Sir, it's not just Rohit. Many of us are struggling to keep up with everything. There's so much work piling up."

Parv chimed in, "Yes, sir! I was up until midnight trying to finish my science project."

"And I stayed up late completing my English essay," added Khushi.

One by one, more students began sharing their stories. Anjali mentioned how she'd been distracted by social media notifications before finally settling down to study. Aman admitted to spending too much time playing video games, which ate into his study hours. Even Namrita, who was usually diligent, confessed that she often found herself procrastinating.

Mr. Soni held up his hand, and the class fell silent again. He walked to the front of the room, leaned against his desk, and looked at the students with a thoughtful expression.

"Let me get this straight," he began. "You're all tired, overwhelmed, and behind on your studies. And why? Because of distractions, procrastination, and a lack of focus. Is that correct?"

The students exchanged nervous glances but nodded in agreement.

Mr. Soni sighed and adjusted his glasses. "Do you know what the root cause of all this is?"

The class stayed silent.

"It's your lack of concentration," he said. "You're unable to focus on what's important because your minds are constantly wandering – to social media, games, or other distractions. And when you do try to study, you find yourself overwhelmed because you've let the work pile up. This cycle of procrastination and stress is entirely of your own making."

Deepika raised her hand timidly. "But, sir, it's so hard to stay focused. There's always something happening online, and it feels impossible to ignore."

"That's precisely the problem," Mr. Soni replied. "You've trained your minds to crave distractions. Every notification, every like, every message—it pulls your attention away from what truly matters. Concentration is a skill, and like any skill, it requires practice."

"But, sir, how do we practice concentration?" Garvit asked. "It's easier said than done."

Mr. Soni smiled knowingly. "I'll tell you a story—a true story—about the power of concentration and how it can change your life. But before that, I want each of you to reflect on how you spend your time. How much of your day is spent scrolling through your phones? How often do you start a task but leave it incomplete because you got distracted? Think about it."

The students fell silent, their heads bowed in thought. Mr. Soni continued, "There was once a person who faced challenges far greater than yours. And yet, he overcame them through sheer focus and determination. He taught us the value of concentration and how it can help us achieve the impossible."

"What happened to him, sir?" Anshika asked, her curiosity piqued.

"I'll tell you, but you must promise me something first," Mr. Soni said, his voice serious.

"What is it, sir?" Gaurav asked.

"Promise me that you'll take this lesson to heart. Promise me that you'll work on improving your concentration and letting go of distractions. If you truly want to succeed, you must learn to focus on what's important and ignore everything else."

The students exchanged glances, then nodded in agreement.

"We promise, sir," they said in unison.

Satisfied, Mr. Soni began his story,

******

In a small, sleepy village in Gujarat, the sun blazed high above, casting long, golden shadows across the earth. The air, thick with the scent of ripe mangoes and freshly tilled soil, buzzed with the hum of everyday life. Women in bright, colorful saris walked to and fro carrying pots of water, and children played in the narrow lanes, their laughter echoing against the clay walls of the village homes.

The villagers had lived simple lives for generations, bound to the land, their days dictated by the seasons. They had little need for the luxuries of the outside world. And, in a place like this, everything moved in harmony with the rhythms of nature. The heartbeat of the village was steady, predictable, and unhurried.

It was on this seemingly normal afternoon that something extraordinary happened. A figure appeared at the village's edge—a sadhu. His saffron robes were stained with blood, and a beige shawl hung loosely around his shoulders. His frail body swayed as he walked, clearly struggling against the pain that radiated from the arrow lodged in his back. The shaft was dark as ebony, protruding at an odd angle, its sharp point glinting in the hot afternoon sun.

The villagers who spotted him stopped in their tracks, whispering amongst themselves. Some crossed themselves; others simply stared, unsure of what to do. The sadhu seemed oblivious to their gazes, his eyes distant, his focus on the Ramji temple that loomed on the outskirts of the village.

The first to notice the sadhu's condition was an elderly woman, her wrinkled face lined with years of labor. She stood by the doorway of her house, clutching a wooden ladle in one hand. Her eyes widened as she saw the bloodstained figure moving toward the temple. "Aye, what happened to him?" she murmured, covering her mouth with her hand.

"Who is that?" another woman asked, her voice tinged with fear. "Is he… is he a ghost?"

"No, no, he's a sadhu," came the reply from an older man, a farmer who had seen many such figures come through the village over the years. "But why is he bleeding like this?"

Before anyone could react, the sadhu staggered closer to the Ramji temple, his steps slow and deliberate. The arrow stuck out of his back like a sinister symbol, its presence jarring against the peaceful atmosphere of the village. When he finally reached the temple steps, he collapsed to the ground, sitting cross-legged with his hands raised in prayer. His face, pale and drawn, remained serene, as though the world around him was fading away.

Inside the temple, the village pundit—a stout man with a thick mustache and a deep, booming voice—was preparing for the afternoon rituals. He was the first to notice the sadhu sitting at the temple steps. His gaze fell upon the blood staining the man's robes, and his face immediately turned pale.

"Who is this?" the pundit muttered to himself, stepping closer. "This is no ordinary sadhu. What happened to him?"

Without wasting a moment, he dashed out of the temple and hurried toward the sadhu. "Arere! What's happened to you, baba?" the pundit asked, bending down to inspect the wound. He saw the arrow lodged deep in the sadhu's back, its barbed edge cruelly embedded in the flesh.

"Someone call the doctor!" the pundit yelled. "Quickly!"

A young man named Jitu, who was gawking curiously nearby, heard the shout and immediately ran toward the nearby house of Vaidh Hariram, the village Ayurveda practitioner. Jitu banged on the wooden door with urgency. "Vaidhji! Vaidhji! Please, hurry!" he called. "A sadhu is sitting outside the temple, and he's been shot! There's an arrow in his back! Please come!"

Vaidh Hariram, a mild-mannered man in his late forties,

was not a man prone to panic, but even he was shaken by the urgency of Jitu's message. He grabbed his medical kit and followed Jitu to the temple. As they approached, the sadhu's form was unmistakable, sitting motionless on the stairs, his hands clasped together, and his head slightly bowed.

"Arre, what is this?" the doctor muttered under his breath, examining the sadhu from a distance. He could see the blood that had pooled around the man's robes, and the arrow that stuck out from his back like a cruel joke. It was impossible to tell how long the sadhu had been suffering, but the doctor knew that it was only a matter of time before the wound turned deadly.

"Doctor sa'ab, what will we do?" Jitu asked, wringing his hands nervously. "We need to remove the arrow!"

Vaidh Hariram nodded, but there was a concern in his eyes. "We must act quickly, but I cannot do it. We would need to send for a surgeon from the city and wait. Also the sadhu is in a meditative state. If we try to remove the arrow now, the shock may kill him."

Listening to Vaidhji's advice the Sarpanch hurried back to his house to contact the Surgeon from the nearby town.

As the hours passed, the anxiety of the villagers kept rising.

Jitu looked at the sadhu, who was still sitting motionless. The blood had not stopped flowing, and yet the man showed no signs of distress. "But he's in pain!" Jitu protested. "We can't wait. He will die if we don't act."

The doctor bent down closer to the sadhu, noticing the quiet breathing that seemed to come from deep within. "No, Jitu, he's not in pain. Look at the calm expression on his face."

"But… but he has an arrow in his back!" Jitu argued, his voice rising in disbelief.

"Sometimes," the doctor said, "there is more to the body than just flesh and blood. Here, the surgeon arrives."

The doctor inspected the wound, he said, "We shall arrange to bring him to the nearby room. Someone, please arrange a cot. We need to operate immediately. I will need to give him anesthesia."

An elderly devotee who had been watching approached the doctor. He was a tall man with a weathered face, his white dhoti flowing gently as he walked.

"Doctor sa'ab," he said, his voice calm, "You cannot give him the sedatives."

The doctor blinked in surprise, "And may I know the reason?"

The devotee smiled gently, "The sadhu's body is his temple. We cannot administer him the drugs"

"But the wound…, Are you insane? Why? He won't be able to bear the pain of removing the arrow."

The man gently suggested, "I'd request you to wait till the evening prayers start. You can operate on him while the prayers are going on. It's just the question of a moment or two now."

"During the prayers? He cannot wait that long." The doctor looked at his patient, wondering how much longer the man could endure.

"In his subconscious mind he has prepared for this, He has gone to the meditative form to bear the pain. He's transcended it. Look at his face—he is not in agony. And once the prayer starts, he would achieve the deepest form of his meditation."

The doctor was hesitant but, sensing the wisdom in the devotee's words, reluctantly agreed. He sat down beside the temple steps and waited with the others as the evening prayers began. The chanting of mantras filled the air, echoing through the village. The sadhu's hands were joined together, and his eyes were closed tight, his breathing had gone deeper and slower. His body, still as a statue, seemed to merge with the sacred vibrations around him.

As the prayers continued, the doctor stood up and approached the sadhu. The villagers, who had gathered to witness the miracle, watched with rapt attention, awe written on their faces. The temple air was thick with devotion, and the light from the oil lamps flickered in the cool evening breeze.

With a steady hand, the doctor moved toward the sadhu and gently grasped the shaft of the arrow. It was surprisingly easy to remove, as though the sadhu's body had already surrendered to the inevitable. Not a sound escaped the sadhu's lips, and not a single muscle twitched. When the doctor pulled the arrow slid out, the blood started flowing more freely as it was freed.

The villagers gasped in disbelief, their eyes wide with wonder. The sadhu remained unchanged, his face a picture of calm and concentration. The doctor worked quickly but carefully, cleaning the wound and bandaging it with the precision of someone who had performed this task countless times. Yet, despite the seriousness of the operation, the sadhu did not flinch, nor did he even seem aware of what was happening.

When the doctor finished, he stepped back, wiping his

brow. The villagers looked at the sadhu, who had not moved a muscle. His face remained peaceful, his breathing steady, and the arrow was gone. The wound was treated and bandaged, but there was no sign of pain, no evidence that the sadhu had endured such an ordeal.

Finally, after what seemed like an eternity, the sadhu slowly opened his eyes. His gaze swept over the villagers, then landed on the doctor. He smiled gently, his eyes sparkling with an inner light. "It is done," he murmured, his voice soft but clear. "The body is healed, the spirit is whole."

The villagers, their hearts full of reverence, watched In silence as the sadhu rose to his feet, steady as a mountain. There was no sign of the pain that had once wracked his body, no trace of the suffering he had endured. Only peace remained.

The pundit, whose eyes were filled with awe, stepped forward and bowed deeply. "In his devotion," he said quietly, "he has shown us the path to true healing. Not just of the body, but of the soul."

The sadhu looked at him, a humble smile playing on his lips. "The body is just a vessel. The soul, however, is eternal."

As the villagers began to leave the temple, their hearts filled with wonder, the sadhu remained behind, sitting quietly in the temple's doorway, his eyes closed once more. And in the soft evening light, the silent miracle of his devotion echoed in their hearts forever.

****

When the story ended, the room erupted in questions.

"Is that really true, sir?" Aman asked.

"Yes," Mr. Soni replied. "And it's proof of what you're capable of when you put your mind to something."

Khushi raised her hand. "Sir, how do we start? How do we improve our concentration?"

"By taking small steps," Mr. Soni said. "See, the sadhu doesn't have any distractions in his life. A sadhu leads an ascetic life, means no worldly distractions, He has forced this lifestyle on himself. You should too do the same. Force yourself to concentrate. Start by setting aside dedicated study time where you turn off all distractions—no phones, no games, no noise. Focus on one task at a time. And most importantly, practice mindfulness. When your mind wanders, bring it back to the task at hand."

The students nodded, their faces thoughtful.

"And remember," Mr. Soni added, "it's not about being perfect. It's about trying every day to be better than you were yesterday. Concentration is like a muscle—the more you exercise it, the stronger it becomes."

The bell rang, signaling the end of class. As the students packed their bags, Rohit approached Mr. Soni hesitantly.

"Sir, I'm sorry for sleeping in your class," he said. "I'll try to focus more and finish my work on time."

Mr. Soni placed a hand on Rohit's shoulder and smiled. "That's all I ask, Rohit. The effort is what matters. Remember, the journey of a thousand miles begins with a single step."

As the students filed out of the classroom, their chatter was filled with plans to improve their focus and take charge of their studies. And as Mr. Soni watched them go, he felt a sense of satisfaction, knowing that he had planted the seeds of change in their young minds.

The lesson was over, but for the students of Class 10, the journey was just beginning.

5

BUDDHA'S GIFTS

The lunch hour was typically a mix of chatter, laughter, and the clinking of tiffin boxes. Mr. Soni, a dedicated teacher known for his calm demeanor, was on lunch duty that day, patrolling the corridors to ensure order. He walked through the hallways, exchanging smiles and quick greetings with students.

Just as he was about to head to the staffroom, two girls came rushing toward him. It was Yana and Krishna, both from Class 9. Their faces were flushed, not from running, but from the weight of something they needed to say.

"Sir, can we talk to you for a moment?" Yana asked, her voice trembling.

"Of course," Mr. Soni said, stepping aside with them. "What's the matter?"

Krishna glanced nervously around to ensure no one was listening. "Sir, it's about Prakriti and Mayra from our class," she began hesitantly.

Mr. Soni frowned slightly. "What about them?"

"They've been using… bad language, sir," Yana interjected. "Cuss words and abusive language, all the time, in the classroom, in front of everyone."

Mr. Soni raised an eyebrow. "And why are they doing this?"

"They think it's funny," Krishna said, her voice growing quieter. "They say it to insult people, to make others laugh. But it's not just jokes, sir. It's really hurtful."

Yana's eyes welled up with tears. "Sir, they use profanities while talking with us too. They always say horrible things… we can't even repeat them."

Mr. Soni's expression softened as he noticed their distress. "I understand this is upsetting," he said gently. "But sometimes, the best thing to do is to ignore such behavior. If you don't give them a reaction, they might stop."

"No, sir," Krishna said, shaking her head. "It's not just us. They say these things to everyone. Some of the boys laugh along, and others feel scared to speak up. It's getting worse."

Yana added, "Please, sir. Do something. We can't handle this anymore."

Mr. Soni sighed, realizing the gravity of the situation. "Alright," he said firmly. "I'll address it during my next lecture with your class. Don't worry, I'll handle it."

The girls nodded, relief washing over their faces, and walked away.

When Mr. Soni entered Class 9-B for his next lecture, he found the atmosphere lively yet chaotic. Prakriti and Mayra were seated in the back, surrounded by a group of boys, laughing loudly. Yana and Krishna sat quietly in the front row, their faces still bearing traces of worry.

Mr. Soni placed his books on the desk and scanned the room. "Good afternoon, everyone," he greeted.

"Good afternoon, sir," the class chorused, though a few voices, including Prakriti's, were delayed and mocking in tone.

Mr. Soni ignored it and began the lecture. After about ten minutes of teaching, he paused, setting his chalk down.

"Class," he said, his tone calm but serious, "I'd like to tell you a story today. It's a story about a man and the Buddha. It's a story about words."

The students perked up. They always enjoyed Mr. Soni's storytelling sessions. Even Prakriti and Mayra quieted down, curious despite themselves.

****

It was a calm afternoon in the serene forests of Magadha. The Buddha sat under a Bodhi tree, surrounded by his disciples. The tranquil atmosphere carried a gentle breeze, and the sound of birdsong intermingled with the rustling of leaves. As the Buddha explained the essence of mindfulness to his followers, a man stormed into the clearing, his face contorted with rage.

"Are you the Buddha?" the man asked, his tone sharp and accusatory.

The Buddha turned to him, his expression serene. "Yes, I am."

Without a moment's hesitation, the man began hurling

insults. "You call yourself enlightened, but you're just another fraud! A hypocrite! You sit here, pretending to be wise, while people waste their time listening to your nonsense!"

The monks exchanged uneasy glances, their discomfort evident. Some whispered among themselves, wondering who this man was and why he spoke with such venom.

"You think you're above everyone else?" the man continued, his voice rising. "You're nothing but a coward, hiding behind your so-called peace and serenity. If you were truly wise, you'd confront the real world instead of sitting here like a useless tree stump!"

The Buddha remained silent, his calm gaze fixed on the man. His lips curled into a faint smile, unshaken by the torrent of abuse.

This silence only seemed to enrage the man further. "Say something!" he demanded. "Defend yourself! Or are you too dumb to even understand what I am saying?"

Ananda, one of the Buddha's closest disciples, couldn't remain silent any longer. "Master," he said softly, leaning closer, "this man is being disrespectful. Shall we ask him to leave?"

The Buddha raised a hand, signaling Ananda to remain calm. "Let him speak," he said gently.

The man laughed mockingly. "Oh, so now you'll let me speak? What a benevolent leader you are!" He scoffed. "You're nothing but a coward who hides behind silence because you have no answers!"

The Buddha finally spoke, his voice calm and composed. "Tell me," he said, "if someone brings a gift to you and you choose not to accept it, to whom does the gift belong?"

The man frowned, caught off guard by the question. "It would still belong to the one who brought it," he said after a pause.

The Buddha nodded. "Exactly. In the same way, if you offer me your anger and insults, and I choose not to accept them, they remain with you."

The man's expression faltered, but his pride wouldn't let him back down. "That's just wordplay!" he retorted. "You can't deny that words have power. My insults must have hurt you, even if you pretend otherwise."

The Buddha's smile deepened. "Words do have power," he agreed. "But only if we allow them to. Imagine someone throws a burning torch at you. If you refuse to catch it, what happens?"

"It falls to the ground," the man admitted reluctantly.

"And who gets burned?" the Buddha asked.

"The one holding the torch," the man muttered, realization beginning to dawn on him.

The Buddha continued, "Your anger is like that burning torch. If I refuse to catch it, it cannot harm me. But as long as you hold onto it, it will burn you from within."

The man shook his head, trying to dismiss the analogy. "But it's not that simple! Anger is a natural reaction. If someone wrongs me, how can I not feel angry?"

"Anger is indeed a natural emotion," the Buddha said. "But it is what you do with that anger that defines you. Consider this: if a snake bites you, do you chase the snake to punish it, or do you focus on treating the wound?"

The man hesitated. "I… I would treat the wound, of course."

"Exactly," the Buddha said. "When someone wrongs you, holding onto anger is like chasing the snake. It distracts you from healing yourself and only prolongs your suffering."

The man folded his arms defensively. "That's easy for you to say. You live in a forest, away from real problems. People in the world don't have the luxury of sitting under a tree and meditating all day."

The Buddha's eyes twinkled with understanding. "Do you believe that challenges only exist in the world outside this forest?"

"Of course!" the man said. "You're sheltered here. You don't deal with betrayal, poverty, or injustice like the rest of us."

The Buddha gestured to a nearby tree. "Do you see this tree?"

"Yes," the man replied, puzzled.

"This tree faces storms, scorching heat, and biting cold. Yet it stands firm, offering shade and shelter to all, without complaint. It does not uproot itself to escape challenges; it remains where it is, enduring and growing stronger. Similarly, peace is not about avoiding challenges—it is about finding strength and calm within them."

The man stared at the tree, then at the Buddha. "But what if people take advantage of your peace? What if they see your calmness as weakness?"

The Buddha smiled. "A tiger does not lose its strength by remaining calm. Peace is not weakness—it is the mastery of strength. When you are at peace, you control your actions, rather than letting your emotions control you."

The man's shoulders slumped, his anger giving way to introspection. "I… I've always let my anger control me," he admitted. "It has caused me more harm than good."

The Buddha placed a hand on the man's shoulder, his touch warm and reassuring. "Recognizing this is the first step toward change. Let go of the burning torch, and you will find freedom."

The man bowed his head, tears welling up in his eyes. "Thank you, Master. Your words have opened my eyes."

The Buddha smiled. "The journey to peace begins within. Take it one step at a time."

The man bowed deeply and left the grove, his heart lighter and his mind clearer than it had been in years. The monks, who had been silent throughout the exchange, looked at the Buddha with awe.

Ananda finally spoke. "Master, your wisdom humbles us all. How do you remain so calm, even in the face of such hostility?"

The Buddha looked at his disciples, his eyes filled with compassion. "When you understand the nature of suffering, you see that anger is only a mask for pain. By responding with compassion, you not only free yourself but also help others find their way."

The monks nodded, their hearts filled with renewed resolve. As the sun dipped lower in the sky, the grove returned to its tranquil state, a testament to the enduring power of peace and wisdom.

****

After finishing the story, Mr. Soni turned to the class, his gaze sweeping across the room. "What do you think this story teaches us?" he asked.

Several hands went up.

"It's about staying calm, sir," Aman said. "Not letting anger take control."

"Exactly," Mr. Soni said. "And it's also about the power of words. Words can hurt as much as actions—sometimes even more. When we use abusive language or insult someone, we're throwing burning torches at them. But what happens when someone refuses to catch that torch?"

"They don't get burned," Garvit answered.

"Correct," Mr. Soni said. "But here's the thing: not everyone can refuse to catch the torch. Some people catch it because they don't know how to ignore it, and they get hurt. And whose fault is that?"

There was silence in the room.

"It's the person who threw the torch," Mayra said softly.

Mr. Soni nodded. "Exactly. When you use hurtful words, you're throwing torches at people. You may think it's just a joke or that it makes you look cool, but you're causing real harm. And the worst part is, those words don't disappear. They linger in people's hearts and minds, sometimes for years."

He paused, letting his words sink in. "Now, I've heard

that some of you have been using such words in this very classroom. Words that hurt, words that divide. I won't name anyone, but I want you to think about this: Is this the kind of person you want to be? Someone who throws torches and burns others?"

Prakriti and Mayra exchanged uneasy glances.

Mr. Soni continued, "It's easy to say things in the heat of the moment or to join in when others are doing it. But it takes real strength to be kind, to speak words that heal rather than hurt. Think about the kind of impact you want to have on the people around you."

The room was silent now, every student deep in thought.

"Words are powerful," Mr. Soni said, his voice softer now. "They can build bridges, or they can destroy them. They can lift someone up, or they can tear them down. The choice is yours. And to those who get hurt by this kind of language, I want to say that they give the words the power by taking them personally and literally. Suppose you are walking on a street and someone calls from behind, 'Ay Donkey, come here.' If you went there, it proves that you are Donkey, but if you had just moved on the Donkey is the one who was talking to the air."

He turned to the blackboard and wrote: "Speak only if it improves upon the silence and listen to everything, but mind only the things useful for you."

"This is something I want you all to remember," he said. "Before you speak, ask yourself: Will my words help someone? Will they bring joy or understanding? If not, maybe it's better to stay silent."

Yana and Krishna looked at each other, their eyes shining with gratitude.

As the bell rang, signaling the end of the period, Mr. Soni gathered his books. "Think about what we discussed today," he said. "The power of words is in your hands. Use it wisely."

The class rose for the customary goodbye, but the usual chatter was absent as the students filed out. Prakriti and Mayra lingered behind, approaching Mr. Soni hesitantly.

"Sir," Mayra said, her voice uncharacteristically quiet, "we… we're sorry."

Prakriti nodded. "We didn't realize how much our words could hurt. We'll try to do better."

Mr. Soni smiled, his faith in his students reaffirmed. "That's all I ask," he said. "Every day is a chance to do better. Use it well."

As they left, the classroom felt lighter, the lesson lingering not just in the air but in their hearts.

6
NARAYAN NARAYAN

The school's multipurpose hall was set up with neatly arranged chairs facing a modest podium. Parents filtered in gradually, some clutching their children's report cards, others with expressions of anticipation and, in some cases, mild apprehension. Mr. Soni stood near the podium, greeting parents with a warm smile as they took their seats.

"Good evening, everyone," he began, tapping the microphone lightly to check the sound. "Thank you for coming. I know how busy all of you are, and it means a lot that you've made time to discuss your child's progress." His voice carried a genuine warmth, putting many of the parents at ease.

He adjusted his glasses and continued, "As you all know, the quarterly exams concluded two weeks ago, and today, we'll be going over your child's results. More importantly, I'd like to discuss how we can work together to prepare them for the upcoming half-yearly exams."

A member of the school staff began distributing report cards. The soft rustle of papers being unfolded soon filled the room, followed by an air of subdued tension as parents reviewed the results.

The silence broke when a mother in a floral saree raised her hand, her voice a mix of concern and frustration. "Mr. Soni, my son's grades in mathematics and science have dropped significantly. He was doing fine last year. What's happening now?"

A father seated near the front chimed in. "My daughter is the same. She's always been good with languages, but her English composition marks this time are...well, disappointing, to say the least."

As murmurs of agreement spread across the room, Mr. Soni raised his hands to gently restore order. "I understand your concerns, and I want to assure you that we are taking this seriously. The purpose of this meeting is not just to share marks but to identify the challenges our students are facing and address them effectively. So let's take a moment to explore what might be causing these performance dips."

The room silenced, save for the sound of a child's faint giggle from a classroom nearby. Mr. Soni took a deep breath and spoke again. "Let me ask you this—how often do you notice your children studying at home?"

A father leaned back in his chair and sighed. "Studying? They're glued to their phones half the time. If it's not social media, it's some online game."

Sir," a tall man in a crisp white shirt began, his voice tinged with frustration. "I'm genuinely concerned about my son. He's always on his phone. Morning, afternoon, night—it doesn't matter. He's either scrolling through social media or glued to some video game. How is he supposed to focus on his studies like this?"

A murmur of agreement swept through the room. Mr. Soni, seated beside the principal, adjusted his glasses and leaned forward, listening intently.

"I completely understand," said a woman wearing a bright yellow saree. "My daughter does the same. She says she's doing her homework, but her earphones are always plugged in, and she's laughing at some video. It's so frustrating!"

Another parent chimed in, his voice a mix of concern and resignation. "It's the same story in every household, sir. These kids are distracted all the time. They don't even sit down for a meal without their phones. It's like they're addicted."

The discussion gathered momentum as more parents voiced their frustrations.

"I would like to ask you all a question," the Principal ma'am said, "Why don't you take away their devices firmly?"

"I tried confiscating the phone," one mother confessed, "but then my son sulked for two days and refused to eat properly."

"Exactly!" said another father. "And even if you take the phone away, there's the TV. Or the tablet. Or the computer. It's like we're fighting a losing battle."

By now, Mr. Soni had filled an entire page with notes. He looked up at the room full of anxious faces and cleared his throat.

"Yes, that's exactly the problem," another parent interjected. "We've tried to set rules about screen time, but it's always a struggle. They get distracted so easily."

Mr. Soni nodded thoughtfully. "It seems distraction is a common thread here. The allure of technology is undeniable, and our children are more susceptible to it than ever. This is not just a home problem—it's something we're observing in school as well. But let me assure you, we can tackle this together."

The parents leaned forward, intrigued.

"My agenda for this meeting was to discuss strategies for preparing your children for the half-yearly exams," Mr. Soni continued, his tone firm yet reassuring. "But it's clear that before we can talk about academics, we need to address the root of the issue—distractions. I believe that the understanding comes from within. I promise you, I will work with your children to help them focus better, both in and outside the classroom. Together, we'll develop a plan that balances their academic needs with their personal interests."

The parents exchanged glances, some visibly relieved, others still skeptical.

"Thank you, Mr. Soni," a mother said. "If anyone can help them, it's you."

As the meeting concluded, Mr. Soni gathered his notes, his mind already racing with ideas for his conversation with the students the next day.

Mr. Soni walked into the classroom the following morning, carrying his leather satchel, a calm but purposeful expression on his face. The students immediately noticed his unusual demeanor.

"Good morning, Sir!" they chorused.

"Good morning," he replied, his voice steady but thoughtful. "Settle down, everyone. We need to talk."

The room grew quiet as the students exchanged curious glances.

"Yesterday, I had a long discussion with your parents during the Parent-Teacher Meeting," Mr. Soni began, placing his satchel on the desk. "Do you know what most of them said about you?"

A few students shifted nervously in their seats. Some looked down, feigning interest in their notebooks.

"They said," Mr. Soni continued, "that you're all incredibly distracted. They talked about your obsession with TV, social media, and games. Is that true?"

"Sir, we always do our homework," a student from the second row piped up.

"Yes, sir, and we submit all assignments on time," added another.

"I'm sure you do," Mr. Soni acknowledged with a nod. "But tell me this—when you're doing your homework, how often do you pick up your phone to check a notification? Or switch tabs to watch a video? How many times does your focus wander while you're supposed to be studying?"

The classroom fell silent. A few students exchanged guilty looks.

"Look," Mr. Soni said, his tone softening, "I'm not here to scold you. Distractions are everywhere—it's not just you. But I want you to understand something important. And for that, let me tell you a story."

He picked up a piece of chalk and drew a simple outline of a bull on the blackboard. The students leaned in, intrigued.

"This is Nandi," he began, turning back to face the class. "The devoted mount of Lord Shiva. And once upon a time…"

****

In the time when humanity was still in its infancy, long before the secrets of agriculture had been unearthed, people lived at the mercy of nature's whims. Forests provided fruits, nuts, and grains, but these were never enough to sustain them, especially during harsh seasons. Food scarcity was a constant shadow looming over their lives, sapping their spirits and forcing them into desperate measures.

The elders of various tribes convened one day in a dry, cracked clearing under a blazing sun. They sat in a circle, their faces etched with worry.

"Our people are starving," one elder lamented, his voice breaking. "Children cry themselves to sleep. The old are too weak to forage. We cannot continue like this."

"There must be a solution," said another. "Perhaps the gods will guide us."

"Yes," agreed a wise woman. "Only the great Mahadev, Lord Shiva, can show us the way. He is our protector, the one who governs both destruction and creation. Let us seek his divine wisdom."

Thus, a delegation of the strongest and wisest was chosen to undertake the perilous journey to Mount Kailasa, Shiva's sacred abode. They trudged for days through treacherous forests, scaling rocky mountains and enduring icy winds that bit at their skin. Finally, they arrived at the celestial peak, their breaths catching at the sight of Shiva seated in serene meditation.

The delegation knelt in reverence. "Mahadev," their leader pleaded, his voice trembling with desperation, "we come seeking your guidance. The Earth no longer provides enough food for us to survive. Please, show us the way."

Shiva opened his eyes slowly, his gaze as deep and steady as the universe itself. "Your suffering does not go unnoticed," he said, his voice carrying both power and compassion. "I will meditate on this matter and seek a solution. Return in a few days, and you shall have your answer."

Relieved and hopeful, the delegation bowed and left. Shiva, the great ascetic, closed his eyes again, plunging into a profound state of meditation. Days passed, during which the mountain air thrummed with divine energy. When Shiva finally emerged, his face shone with the radiance of newfound wisdom.

He summoned Nandi, his loyal bull and ever-faithful servant. Nandi approached, bowing low. "What is your command, my Lord?"

"Nandi," Shiva said, his tone grave, "I have found the solution to humanity's plight. Deliver this message to the people of Earth: 'Once to eat and thrice to bathe.' This practice will restore balance and harmony."

"As you wish, Mahadev," Nandi replied, his chest swelling with pride.

With the message clear in his mind, Nandi set off immediately, his hooves striking the ground with purpose. He repeated the words aloud as he went: "Once to eat and thrice to bathe… once to eat and thrice to bathe."

But as he made his way down the divine path, a familiar figure appeared before him in a burst of celestial light.

"Narayan, Narayan!" exclaimed Narada, the ever-curious and mischievous sage. Veena in hand, Narada floated down to block Nandi's path. "And where are you off to in such haste, dear Nandi?"

"I am on an urgent mission for Lord Shiva," Nandi replied, his voice firm.

"A mission, you say?" Narada's eyes sparkled with curiosity. "Do tell me more!"

"I am carrying a message to the people of Earth," Nandi said, trying to move past.

But Narada wasn't one to let an opportunity for gossip slip by. "Oh, but surely you can spare a moment for an old friend!" he insisted, his tone playful. "Besides, you look like you've been working far too hard. A little break won't hurt."

Nandi hesitated. Narada was persistent, and before Nandi realized what was happening, they were engaged in a lengthy conversation about celestial gossip, the latest happenings in the heavens, and even Nandi's coat grooming secrets.

By the time Narada left with a satisfied chuckle, Nandi's focus had blurred. His mantra, once clear and precise, now wavered in his mind.

When he finally reached the Earth, Nandi raised his voice and declared, "Once to bathe and thrice to eat! This is Lord Shiva's solution to your troubles."

The people, trusting Nandi implicitly, began following the new instructions. They ate more and bathed less, but instead of solving the food scarcity, it only worsened. Their resources dwindled further, and despair returned.

Determined to find answers, the people climbed Mount Kailasa once again. Bowing before Shiva, they cried, "Mahadev, your solution has failed us! The Earth's bounty is more depleted than ever."

Shiva frowned, his divine aura darkening like a storm cloud. "That cannot be," he said. "Nandi!"

Nandi approached, his head hanging low. "Yes, my Lord?"

"What message did you deliver?" Shiva asked, his voice calm but firm.

Nandi stammered, "I told them… 'Once to bathe and thrice to eat.'"

Shiva's eyes widened in disbelief. "You reversed my words! I said, 'Once to eat and thrice to bathe!'"

Realizing his grave mistake, Nandi fell to his knees. "Forgive me, Mahadev," he pleaded. "Narada distracted me, and I lost my focus."

Shiva sighed, his anger softening into pity. "Mistakes are a part of learning, but this one has caused great suffering. To atone, you and your descendants will help humanity cultivate food. From now on, bulls will plow the fields, ensuring that no one goes hungry again."

From that day onward, bulls became humanity's steadfast partners in farming, tilling the soil and helping grow the food that sustains life.

****

When Mr. Soni finished the tale of Nandi, the classroom was silent. The students sat still, processing the story's meaning.

"So," Mr. Soni said, breaking the silence, "what do you think Nandi's mistake teaches us?"

Prachi, sitting near the window, raised her hand. "That… we should pay attention to what we're doing. And make sure we get it right."

"Good," Mr. Soni said, nodding. "But let's take it deeper. What caused Nandi to make that mistake?"

"Distraction," Riya said after a moment of thought. "Narad Muni distracted him with all the gossip."

"Exactly!" Mr. Soni exclaimed, his voice firm but encouraging. "Nandi's devotion to Lord Shiva and his task was unquestionable. But even the most focused can falter when they let distractions creep in. And that one small misstep caused widespread confusion and suffering."

He walked to the blackboard and wrote in bold letters: Distraction ≠ Relaxation

"Now, let me ask you this: how many of you sit down to study but end up scrolling through Instagram or texting friends within five minutes?"

A few hesitant hands went up. Others exchanged nervous glances, knowing they were guilty too.

"I thought so," Mr. Soni said with a chuckle. "And how many of you tell yourselves, 'Oh, I'll just watch one episode,' and then suddenly, it's midnight, and your homework isn't done?"

This time, almost everyone laughed, their embarrassment evident.

"You see, the problem isn't just the distractions themselves," Mr. Soni continued, his tone growing serious. "It's that you've allowed them to take priority over what's important. Nandi's mistake was a one-time event, but for many of you, distractions have become a habit. And habits, good or bad, shape your future."

"But sir," Hardik said from the back, "it's not like we don't want to study. It's just hard to ignore the notifications or stop binge-watching once we start."

"I understand, Hardik," Mr. Soni replied, nodding empathetically. "It has always been the thing with social media. Narada himself represents the Social Media. In the Greek culture Hermes plays that role. Its job is to come to you when you need to concentrate the most on the task at hand. And I'm not asking you to give up your phones or TV entirely. Balance is the key. Let me show you how."

He turned back to the blackboard and wrote:
1. Prioritize: Decide what's most important. Your studies should come first during the day.

2. Set Boundaries: Allocate specific times for relaxation, like watching TV or using social media, but stick to them.

3. Create a Study Routine: A consistent schedule helps your brain focus better.

4. Minimize Temptations: Keep your phone in another room or use apps that block distractions while you study.

"Think of this as your personal Nandi mantra," he said, smiling. "If Nandi had stuck to his task without letting Narad Muni distract him, he wouldn't have made that mistake. Similarly, if you stick to your priorities, you'll see better results—not just in school, but in life."

"But what if we slip up again?" Riya asked, her voice tinged with worry.

"That's a fair question," Mr. Soni said, leaning against his desk. "Mistakes are natural. Even Nandi, who was the most loyal and focused, made one. The important thing is to recognize when you've gone off track and correct it. You're not competing with anyone else—just aim to be a little better than you were yesterday."

Lakshit raised his hand hesitantly. "Sir, what if we try, but the distractions still feel stronger than our willpower?"

Mr. Soni smiled warmly. "That's when you ask for help, from your parents, your teachers, or even your friends. Remember, you're not alone in this. We're here to guide you, just like Lord Shiva helped Nandi find a solution."

The class nodded in unison, their faces reflecting a mix of determination and hope.

"Alright, let's make a deal," Mr. Soni said, looking around the room. "For the next week, I want each of you to try this mantra. Focus on your studies, set boundaries for your distractions, and see how it changes things. Whenever you pick up the phone to check on Instagram, just remember, 'Success is in the work you are avoiding.' At the end of the week, we'll discuss what worked and what didn't. Are we agreed?"

"Yes, sir!" the class chorused enthusiastically.

"Good," Mr. Soni said, a satisfied smile spreading across his face. "Now, let's make sure Nandi's lesson wasn't in vain. The road to success is long, but trust me—it's worth every step."

As the bell rang and the students packed up their bags, there was a renewed sense of purpose in the air. For the first time in a long while, the distractions seemed conquerable, and the path to progress felt clear.

7
THE GHOST OF THE TAMARIND

It was a warm afternoon, and the faint hum of the ceiling fan filled the sixth-class classroom. The students were restless, their usual energy amplified by the absence of Sunder Sir, who was on leave that day. When Mr. Soni walked into the room as their substitute, the students erupted into cheers.

"Mr. Soni! Mr. Soni!" they called out with infectious enthusiasm.

He chuckled, setting his notebook on the teacher's desk. "Alright, alright, settle down, everyone!"

The class quickly quietened, their eager faces looking up at him.

"Well, since Sunder Sir isn't here today," Mr. Soni began, "we've got two whole periods together. What shall we do?"

"Story! Story! Story!" the students chanted in unison, their excitement contagious.

Mr. Soni laughed, shaking his head in mock defeat.

"Alright, you win. But tell me, what kind of story do you want to hear?"

Suggestions flew in from all corners of the room.

"Akbar-Birbal!" shouted one.

"BTS adventures!" another chimed in, earning some giggles.

"Tenalirama!" suggested a girl from the back.

"Ninja Hattori!" a boy yelled, his voice full of hope.

But then, a boy named Rohan jumped up, almost knocking over his desk in his excitement. "Sir, is there a ghost in real life?"

The room fell silent for a split second before erupting into chatter.

"Ghosts are real!" one student declared confidently.

"No, they're not!" another countered.

"My papa says ghosts are just made-up stories to scare kids!" a boy named Aarav said, crossing his arms.

Mr. Soni held up his hand, signaling for silence. The room gradually quieted down, every eye fixed on him.

He raised an eyebrow and asked, "How many of you think ghosts are real?"

A few hands shot up enthusiastically, while others hesitated.

"And how many of you think they aren't?" he continued.

Aarav raised his hand confidently. "My papa says they don't exist!"

Mr. Soni smiled knowingly, leaning forward. "Well, Aarav, what your papa said reminds me of a story. Why don't we listen to it, and then all of you can decide for yourselves whether ghosts are real or not?"

The students leaned in, their curiosity piqued. "Yes, sir! Tell us!" they chorused.

Mr. Soni cleared his throat, his face taking on a mysterious expression. "Alright then. Let me take you to a little village, long ago, where a boy had a very peculiar encounter…"

The students were hooked, their imaginations already racing.

****

Has it ever happened to you that you're with someone, having a perfectly normal conversation, and suddenly the other person goes silent, starts making random gestures, or makes strange noises?

How would you feel in that moment? Confused? Maybe even a little alarmed?

I was in seventh grade then. My family had recently moved to a completely new area on the outskirts of the city. It wasn't just a new house—it was a new world for me, with different faces, unfamiliar streets, and a distinct sense of isolation.

Two or three weeks after settling in, my mom and I went to the local market one sunny afternoon. The hustle and bustle of the marketplace felt like a festival of colors and sounds. The vegetable vendors yelled out their prices, carts loaded with fruits creaked under their weight, and children ran around carrying balloons.

On our way back, my hands were laden with two heavy bags—one stuffed with vegetables, the other with fruits. It's a role every Indian boy knows too well. When you accompany your mother to the market, you're not just a companion; you're the designated bag carrier.

As we walked home, I was chatting animatedly about my new school, friends, and teachers. I was telling my mom about how our math teacher always wore mismatched socks, how the canteen's samosas were the best, and how I managed to score full marks on a geography quiz.

And then it happened.

We were near Savita Ajji's house when my mom, mid-sentence, went completely silent. Her pace didn't falter; she kept walking, but something about her demeanor had changed.

At first, I thought she was just lost in thought. But then she started making strange noises from her throat, almost like someone clearing their voice—except it was continuous and rhythmic.

"Hmm-mmm-hmm," she went, her eyes darting toward me, then toward the path ahead.

Her hand gestures became frantic. She waved her arm as if swatting an invisible fly, then pressed her finger firmly against her lips. When that didn't work, she did something even more peculiar—she touched her nose, signaling me to stop talking.

I stared at her, baffled. What on earth was going on?

Once we cleared the lane, my mom let out a sigh of relief. She slapped me lightly on the back of my head—not enough to hurt, but enough to let me know I'd done something wrong.

She finally spoke, her voice low but firm. "Are you out of your mind? Didn't you see that tamarind tree over there?"

"Yeah, I saw it," I said, thoroughly confused. "But so what? How is that relevant?"

Uh-oh.

Now, let me explain something about Indian culture. There are nearly 5,000 species of trees in India, but only a select few are featured in the ghost stories parents tell their children:

The Banyan tree,

The Peepal tree,

And, of course, the Tamarind tree.

Maybe it's their sheer size or their eerie silhouettes at night that make them prime candidates for supernatural lore. But I, being a naïve seventh-grader, had no idea about this vital piece of cultural knowledge.

Questions began swirling in my mind:

Where exactly do ghosts live? In the trunk? The branches? The leaves? Or maybe... in the fruit?

What happens if I eat a tamarind with a ghost in it?

How do people even know if a tree is haunted?

I turned to my mom, eager for answers.

She sighed as if preparing for a lecture. "Listen carefully," she began, her tone serious. "Ghosts live in tamarind trees. They don't bother you unless you invite them."

"Invite them? How?" I asked, my curiosity piqued.

"If you use certain words—like 'come' or 'let's go'—the ghost will follow you. And once it follows you, it won't leave until it consumes you or possesses you."

Her explanation only raised more questions.

"How would I know if a ghost is following me?" I asked, my voice tinged with apprehension.

"You'll hear the sound of its ghoonghroo," she replied.

"Do male ghosts also wear ghoonghroo?"

"No," she said matter-of-factly. "Male ghosts are so heavy that when they walk, the ground trembles."

"How many ghosts can possess a person at once?"

My mom hesitated for a moment before answering, "There was a distant relative of ours who was possessed by eleven ghosts at the same time. He couldn't speak, couldn't eat, couldn't sleep—it was terrible."

Her answers were so detailed, so convincing, that I couldn't help but believe her. From that day onward, I adopted a new rule: whenever we passed that lane, I would clamp my mouth shut and walk as quickly as possible, my eyes fixed firmly on the ground.

For a seventh-grader, it was better to be safe than sorry.

That silence about ghosts and the tamarind tree lasted until one fateful day during Mr. Pravin Waghmare's class.

Now, Mr. Waghmare wasn't just any teacher—he was a force to reckon with. With his booming voice and razor-sharp logic, he could make you doubt everything from astrology to why you even needed an extra notebook for rough work. He was also a proud member of an anti-superstition group and loved picking apart any belief he deemed irrational.

That day, as we were wrapping up a lively discussion on myths and folklore, he said with absolute certainty, "There's no such thing as ghosts."

The classroom fell into an awkward silence. A few of my classmates exchanged nervous glances. It was as though Mr. Waghmare had just insulted our collective childhoods.

I, however, couldn't let that slide. Before I could stop myself, my hand shot up.

"Yes, Soni?" he said, his eyes narrowing slightly. "Do you have something to add?"

I stood up, my chair scraping loudly against the floor. "Sir, my mother says there are ghosts. And one of them lives in the tamarind tree near my house. It follows people if you call it."

The class collectively sucked in their breath. Some giggled, while others whispered, "Tamarind tree? Of course, it had to be a tamarind tree!"

Mr. Waghmare crossed his arms and leaned against his desk. "Follows people, you say? And how does this ghost… follow them, exactly?"

"Well," I began, "my mom says it follows if you use certain words, like 'come' or 'let's go.' And it doesn't stop until it's, um… possessed you."

He raised an eyebrow. "Possessed you? Interesting! So, have you been possessed by this ghost yet?"

"No," I admitted, "but my mom says—"

"Ah," he cut me off, holding up a finger. "Your mom says. But have you seen this ghost? Or heard it? Any ghoonghroos? Heavy footsteps?"

"Well, no. But—"

"Exactly," he interrupted again, pacing the front of the room now. "You haven't seen it. You haven't heard it. You haven't experienced it. And yet, you believe it because someone told you so?"

"Yes," I replied stubbornly. "Because my mom said it."

The class burst into laughter, but I stood my ground.

Mr. Waghmare chuckled. "Soni, let me explain something to you. There's a little thing called evidence. You can't just believe in something without proof. Ghosts, for example. No one has ever photographed a ghost, recorded a ghost, or scientifically proven a ghost exists. Do you understand?"

"But sir," I argued, "just because no one's seen something doesn't mean it isn't real! We can't see air, but we know it's there!"

The class erupted into applause. Even I felt a small swell of pride.

"Nice try," he said, smirking. "But air is real. We can

measure it, feel it, and study it. Ghosts, on the other hand? Pure imagination."

"But sir," I shot back, "how do you explain the stories of people being possessed? Or hearing strange noises at night?"

"Ah, stories." He tapped his temple dramatically. "Stories, my dear Soni, are born from fear and ignorance. People hear noises or see shadows, and their minds conjure up ghosts to explain what they don't understand."

"But what about my mom's story of the tamarind tree ghost? She told me it has followed people before!"

"And have those people come to me with any evidence?" he asked, spreading his arms theatrically. "I'll wait. Until then, here's my challenge to you: go and see this ghost. Find proof. And if you can, come back and tell me all about it."

The room buzzed with excitement. A few kids whispered, "Are you really going to do it, Soni?"

I nodded firmly, though my insides were twisting. "I'll do it, sir. I'll prove it to you."

Mr. Waghmare grinned, clearly enjoying the show. "Well then, good luck. And remember: no evidence, no ghosts."

There's a proverb in Gujarati language about not giving a monkey a ladder, but Mr. Waghmare gave me one. And boy, did I climb it!

That evening, I hatched a plan.

At precisely 7 o'clock, I grabbed my football, attempting to look as casual as possible. "I'm going to play, Ma," I called out over the sounds of yet another dramatic confrontation in her favorite soap opera.

"Hmmm," she murmured distractedly, her eyes glued to the TV screen where the protagonist was either fainting, or crying, or perhaps discovering a long-lost sibling. Perfect. I could've told her I was heading to Mars, and she wouldn't have noticed.

Grabbing my little Hercules bike, my pride and joy, I pedaled toward the tamarind tree, adrenaline coursing through my veins.

The street was eerily quiet. Most neighbors were indoors finishing their dinners or preparing for their evening prayers. The tamarind tree loomed at the end of the lane, its crooked branches reaching out like dark, skeletal fingers. The chilly December breeze rustled its leaves, making them whisper secrets to the night.

My heart raced. For a moment, I considered turning back. But then, Mr. Waghmare's mocking words echoed in my mind: "No evidence, no ghosts."

Oh, I'll get you your evidence, sir.

I parked my bike across the lane, strategically positioning it for a quick escape. It leaned against the wall of Savita Ajji's villa, the perfect spectator for my bravery—or stupidity.

Taking a deep breath, I approached the tree.

"Alright," I whispered to myself, "this is it."

I stood a few feet away from the trunk, my legs trembling slightly. No big deal, just summoning a ghost. Totally normal seventh-grader activity.

"Ye re," I whispered, my voice so soft it barely reached my own ears. (In Marathi, "Ye re" means "come.")

And then I ran.

I mean, bolted—back to my bike as if my life depended on it. My hands clutched the handlebars, my ears straining for any sound: ghoonghroos, heavy footsteps, the tree's branches creaking ominously.

Nothing.

Maybe the ghost didn't hear me. Or maybe it was shy.

Alright, time for Round Two.

I stepped closer to the tree this time, the crunch of gravel under my shoes echoing in the stillness. The trunk looked bigger now, its rough bark glinting faintly in the dim streetlight.

"YE RE!" I said, louder this time, my voice cracking slightly.

And once again, I ran.

Back to the bike. My heart was pounding like a drumline at a festival. I stared at the tree, half-expecting it to uproot itself and start chasing me.

Still nothing.

I narrowed my eyes. "Alright, Mr. Ghost, you asked for this."

I strode closer, emboldened by the lack of supernatural activity. This time, I stood directly under the tree, craning my neck to look up into its canopy. The branches swayed gently, as if mocking me.

"YE RE!" I bellowed, the loudest yet.

And then… silence.

No ghoonghroos. No whispers. No eerie gust of wind. The only thing that moved was a lone squirrel darting across a branch, pausing to stare at me like I'd lost my mind.

By now, my fear had turned into sheer irritation.

"Alright, ghost," I muttered, hands on my hips. "What are you doing up there? Knitting? Sleeping? Watching cricket? You're supposed to haunt me!"

The squirrel blinked, unimpressed.

I yelled again, my voice echoing in the empty street. "YE RE! Are you even listening? Don't make me climb up there and get you myself!"

Nothing. Not even a suspicious rustling of leaves.

With each attempt, I grew bolder. I went to and fro, from the tree to my bike several times. After every shout, I dashed back to my bike like a seasoned sprinter in a bizarre relay race, ready to flee at the slightest hint of ghoonghroo sounds.

I must've shouted "YE RE!" more than a dozen times by the end, raising my voice an octave with each attempt.

By the end of it, I wasn't scared anymore. I was annoyed.

Frustrated, I stomped back to my bike. "Lazy ghost," I grumbled, shaking my head. "Probably on strike or something."

But deep down, I knew what this meant.

Either the ghost was the laziest specter in existence, or—just as Mr. Waghmare had said—there were no ghosts at all.

Feeling triumphant, I hopped onto my bike, pedaling home with a grin stretched across my face. As I neared my house, I imagined myself in class the next day, standing proudly in front of Mr. Waghmare.

No ghosts, sir. Mission accomplished.

Little did I know, my real adventure with the tamarind tree wasn't over just yet.

When I returned home, I declared to my mom with bravado, "What, Ma? You're such a scaredy-cat. There's no ghost in that tamarind tree. No one even responds when you call!"

Her eyes narrowed. She tilted her head, turned her neck slowly toward me (you could almost hear the creak of an old iron gate), and asked in a dangerously calm voice, "What did you do? Where did you go?"

I told her everything.

For a moment, she didn't say a word. Then, to my surprise, she smiled—a smile that, looking back, should have been my warning. She rose from her chair and sauntered into the kitchen. She started banging and clattering the utensils as if she was trying to find out something frantically.

Then after a minute or two she came out, with the house broom in her hand.

"Ah," I thought, "she's going to sweep the floor."

What followed is a part of my life I've chosen to forget. The broom wasn't used for cleaning that day.

"What were you thinking?!" she thundered, brandishing the broom like a knight with a sword.

"I—uh—I was just experimenting," I stammered, backing away.

"Experimenting? With ghosts? At night? Near the tamarind tree?!"

"B-but, Ma, there's no such thing as ghosts!"

WHACK!

"That's for going to the tamarind tree."

WHACK!

"That's for calling ghosts like some village tantrik!"

WHACK!

"And that's for thinking you know better than your mother!"

About two weeks later, just as the welts from my mom's "disciplinary action" had faded and my ghost experiment was a distant memory, there was a knock at the door.

It was Savita Ajji, carrying her signature basket of guavas.

"Arrey, Ajji! What a pleasant surprise!" my mom exclaimed. "Come, sit. How have you been? You haven't come around for so many days."

Ajji settled on the sofa with a sigh, placing the basket on the table. "I've been under the weather, beta. I had a fever for a week. But I'm fine now, so don't worry."

"What happened, Ajji? Why did you fall sick all of a sudden?"

Ajji adjusted her saree and leaned forward, her voice dropping to a conspiratorial whisper. "It was two weeks ago, one evening," she said. "I was in the yard, resting, when I heard someone calling me from the tamarind tree across my house. It was your Ajjoba (grandpa) —I'm sure of it."

The guava I was munching on nearly fell from my hand. As far as I am concerned I knew she was a widow since last ten years.

"What do you mean, Ajji?" my mom asked, her tone cautious but curious.

Ajji's face softened with nostalgia. "You know, when I was young, your grandpa always wanted to install a proper garden swing set in our compound. But money was tight, so he'd tie a handmade swing made of ropes and old scooter tyre to that tamarind's branch. He'd sit on it and call me, 'Ye re,' inviting me to swing with him."

Her voice cracked as she continued, "That night, I heard the same call—'Ye re' over and over. It was him. He was calling me. I'm sure of it. He's waiting for me."

A cold shiver ran down my spine. The weight of her words, combined with the timing, struck me like a thunderbolt. My heart sank deeper with every passing second. Only now I started realising how ghosts were MADE.

I wished I could have explained to her, but alas! I dared

not look up at my mom. I could feel her gaze boring into me like lasers. My hands mechanically flipped the pages of my textbook as if that would save me from her wrath.

Ajji wiped her tears and smiled. "Anyway, I just wanted to see you all. Here, kiddo, have some guavas. You like them, don't you?"

"Y-yes, Ajji. Thank you," I stammered, my voice barely audible.

After Ajji left, my mom turned to me, her expression a mix of anger, exasperation, and something bordering on "I told you so."

I braced myself for the inevitable confrontation. "Should I tell her?" I asked.

"Don't you realize how much pain you have already given her?" she asked in a voice colder than the December night air. "What are you going to tell her? "There is no such thing as ghost or the 'Grandpa' for that matter?"

"I—uh—I was just…"

"Yes? Tell me. Do go on…" she prompted, raising an eyebrow threateningly.

But, thankfully, before I could dig my grave any deeper, the doorbell rang again, distracting her.

I didn't waste a moment. I grabbed my textbooks and bolted to my room, locking the door behind me. I may have escaped the immediate consequences, but the weight of guilt and a newfound respect for the mysterious tamarind tree stayed with me for a long, long time.

Two weeks later, I was a part of the funeral procession of

Savita Ajji. I couldn't give her my shoulder being a child, but the weight of her bier was on my heart.

Years later when I had completed my 10th standard, my papa bought a big house in a more developed part of the city, far from the dusty lanes and familiar streets I had grown accustomed to. Moving meant new opportunities, new schools, and new beginnings. But it also meant leaving behind pieces of the life I had quietly cherished, even the tamarind tree that had haunted and fascinated me for years.

The evening the movers packed up all our belongings, I sent my parents ahead to the new house. "I want to meet my friends one last time," I told them. It wasn't entirely a lie, but my real purpose wasn't to say goodbye.

While packing, I had found an old scooter tire buried deep in the storeroom, its surface cracked but sturdy. Alongside it, a length of rope had caught my eye. Together, they sparked an idea—a final gesture for the tamarind tree.

As twilight painted the sky in hues of amber and violet, I carried the tire and rope to the tree. Its branches stretched like ancient arms, silhouetted against the fading light, swaying gently as if beckoning me closer. The air was cool and carried the faint scent of earth and tamarind pods.

I climbed onto the lower branch, knotting the rope tightly around it and fastening the scooter tire to make a crude swing. It creaked as it settled into place, dangling there like a child's forgotten dream.

Satisfied, I jumped down and sat with my back resting against the thick trunk of the tree, watching the swing sway gently in the breeze. For a moment, I felt a strange contentment. Maybe, I thought, something as innocent as a child's swing could soften the eerie reputation of this place.

The sun dipped below the horizon, and the sky darkened. Shadows stretched long and deep, blurring the edges of the world. The swing rocked slowly, creaking in rhythm with the whisper of the wind. I closed my eyes, soaking in the moment, the cool bark pressing against my back.

Then, I felt it—a hand on my shoulder.

Warm, light, unmistakably human. I could even see it with my peripheral vision. And old woman's hand with brown , dry, thin and wrinkled skin.

I froze.

Before I could move, a soft, familiar voice spoke behind me, so close it sent shivers racing down my spine. "Hey, kiddo, peru khayche ka?"

My breath caught.

The tone, the warmth, the exact words I had heard countless times. But it couldn't be her, Could it?

My mind raced. My back was pressed firmly against the tree trunk—it was too thick for anyone to be behind me. There was no space, no possibility.

I stood up abruptly, my heart pounding in my ears. The swing swayed, creaking softly, as if mocking my fear.

I didn't look back.

I couldn't dare.

With trembling steps, I started walking away from the tamarind tree, and tripped on the root poking out of the ground. My knee got scratched and it was burning like hell.

But I got up. I didn't run, though every fiber of my being screamed at me to. The voice lingered in the air, faint and fading, as though it came from a distant world.

When I reached the main road, I turned once to glance back. The swing swayed in the wind, and the tree stood still, its shadow merging with the night.

I never went back. Some mysteries are better left unsolved."

****

After delivering the thrilling conclusion of his story about the ghost of the tamarind tree, Mr. Soni paused for a moment, his gaze drifting over the sea of young, wide-eyed faces in front of him. The classroom was eerily quiet, the usual buzz of chatter replaced by a stunned silence. It was as if the students were still processing the unsettling climax, their young minds grappling with the tale's suspenseful intricacies.

Finally, one brave soul broke the silence. A boy sitting in the second row raised his hand, his eyes filled with a mix of curiosity and fear. "Sir… didn't you see her face? The ghost's face?"

Mr. Soni leaned forward, resting his hands on the desk at the front of the classroom. "That's the strange part, isn't it? I never dared to look back. I could feel her presence, though, like the weight of her gaze pressing down on me. But sometimes, not knowing makes it all the more terrifying, don't you think?"

The boy shivered visibly, but before he could respond, another student chimed in, "Is that a real story, sir? Or are you just making it up to scare us?"

Mr. Soni chuckled softly. "Ah, that's the question, isn't it?

What do you think? Is the story real, or is it just my imagination playing tricks on me? Let's just say that some stories are best left open to interpretation."

A girl in the back of the room raised her hand, her brow furrowed in thought. "Sir, why didn't you go back there? To the tamarind tree?"

Mr. Soni's expression turned thoughtful. "Because sometimes, the fear we carry from a moment like that lingers long after the moment itself has passed. I was your age back then, and the memory of that evening haunted me for years. It wasn't just about the ghost; it was about what it represented—something unknown, something I didn't fully understand."

The questions began to pour in, the children unable to contain their excitement and curiosity any longer.

"Are you still afraid of the ghost?"

"Do you think the Ajji became the ghost?"

"Didn't she follow you?"

With each question, Mr. Soni took his time to answer, weaving a mix of logic and mystery into his responses.

"Fear isn't something we ever fully outgrow," he admitted. "It changes shape, takes on new forms, but it always teaches us something. And about Ajji? Well… who knows? People have their own ways of staying connected to places and memories. Maybe that was her way of holding on."

The students listened intently, their Imaginations running wild. A boy in the front, who had been silent until now, finally spoke up. "Sir, do you think ghosts are real?"

Mr. Soni smiled, his eyes twinkling with a mixture of playfulness and mystery. "Real or not, a good story can make you believe, even if just for a moment. And that's what matters."

The bell rang, signaling the end of the period, but the students lingered, their curiosity still buzzing. As Mr. Soni packed his things and prepared to leave, he glanced back at the classroom.

"Think about it, kids," he said with a wink. "Maybe the scariest ghosts aren't the ones hiding in trees, but the ones we carry inside us."

And with that, he walked out, leaving behind a room full of students who, for the first time, weren't quite so sure about the world they thought they knew.

8
PRACTICE MAKES A MAN PERFECT

One Week after the Half-Yearly Exams the classroom buzzed with restless energy as students slumped over their desks, staring at their exam results. A palpable tension hung in the air, punctuated by the occasional rustling of papers or the sniffle of a student on the verge of tears. The once lively classroom, with its posters of inspirational quotes and colorful charts on the walls, felt unusually heavy that day.

Mr. Soni, the class teacher, stood at his desk, his arms folded as he observed the somber faces before him. His heart sank at the sight of his students—these young minds he had nurtured—feeling so defeated.

He cleared his throat and said, "Alright, class, let's talk about it. What's going on?"

For a moment, silence reigned. Then, one brave soul, Akash, raised his hand. His face, usually animated with curiosity, now bore a shadow of disappointment.

"Sir," he began hesitantly, "we tried. We really did. But our marks... they're so bad."

The class murmured in agreement. Rajshree, sitting in the front row, added in a trembling voice, "It's not that we don't want to do well, sir. We study hard, but nothing seems to stay in our heads."

A ripple of agreement followed her words, and Mr. Soni's gaze softened.

"I see," he said, nodding. "So, it's not just about the effort—it's about memory. Is that right?"

"Yes, sir," Rajshree replied, her voice barely above a whisper. "We revise, but when the exam comes, it's like everything just disappears."

At the back of the room, Aditya raised his hand. "Sir, I read my notes again and again, but it doesn't help. I just can't seem to remember things when I need to."

Another boy, Karni Pratap, chimed in, his frustration evident. "And it's not just during exams, sir. Even when we're doing homework, it feels like all the studying was for nothing. I keep forgetting what I've already learned."

Mr. Soni took a deep breath, his mind racing. These weren't just complaints; they were cries for help from students who genuinely wanted to do better but didn't know how.

He stepped away from his desk and walked slowly down the aisle, his hands clasped behind his back. "How many of you feel this way, that no matter how hard you study, you just can't retain the information?"

Every hand in the classroom shot up, some more hesitantly than others.

Mr. Soni stopped in his tracks and turned to face the

class. "First, let me say this: You are not alone. This is a problem many students face—not just in this school, but everywhere. And the good news is, it's something we can work on together. But first like always, How about a tiny story first?"

The students sat up a little straighter, their curiosity piqued. Atmosphere was suddenly charged with newfound anticipation. Seeing the agreement on their faces Mr. Soni continued,

****

Long ago, in the heart of a verdant valley, nestled among mist-covered hills, stood an ashram that radiated wisdom and discipline. The ashram, surrounded by dense groves of mango and neem trees, was a sanctuary for learning. It's simple stone structures with thatched roofs were built to harmonize with the natural surroundings. The faint fragrance of jasmine and sandalwood lingered in the air, mingling with the rhythmic chants of students reciting shlokas, their voices rising and falling like a sacred hymn to the heavens.

The ashram was not just a center of academic learning but a way of life. Every dawn began with the melodious call of a conch shell, followed by hours of meditation and yoga under the sprawling canopy of an ancient banyan tree. The students, clad in saffron dhotis, engaged in rigorous physical training, practiced agricultural chores, and learned the Vedas, philosophy, and astronomy. Their days were structured, filled with tasks that fostered discipline and humility, while the nights were spent in quiet contemplation or storytelling by the fire.

The Guru, an elderly man with a flowing white beard and eyes that seemed to hold the wisdom of the universe, presided over the ashram with an air of calm authority. His presence was like the stillness of a deep river—serene yet powerful. His teachings were revered, and the students clung to his words as if they were lifelines.

Among these students was Budhiya, a boy of about thirteen summers, whose simple appearance and earnest demeanor set him apart. Unlike his peers, Budhiya's grasp of academics was slow. While others solved arithmetic problems with ease or recited verses flawlessly, Budhiya often stumbled, needing repeated explanations.

"Budhiya," one of his teachers sighed during a lesson on Sanskrit grammar, "how many times must I explain this? It's as if your mind is made of stone!"

The other boys snickered, their laughter a mixture of amusement and pity. Budhiya's cheeks burned with embarrassment, but he said nothing. He was used to such remarks. Yet, he bore no grudge against his peers or teachers. He believed in the words his mother had whispered to him on the day he left for the ashram:

"Budhiya, respect your teachers. Follow their instructions with full dedication. Remember, the path of learning is never easy, but your sincerity will guide you."

Each evening, as the students gathered under the banyan tree for their simple meals of rice and lentils, Budhiya sat quietly, listening to their chatter but rarely contributing. He had no grand stories of achievement to share. His days were a constant struggle to keep up, and yet, he remained steadfast in his efforts.

One afternoon, as the sun blazed in the sky, Budhiya's struggles tested the patience of his teacher, who was already dealing with personal frustrations.

"Budhiya!" the teacher snapped after yet another mistake in recitation. "Do you have no sense? How many times must

I tell you? Even a donkey learns faster than you!"

The class erupted in laughter, but the teacher's next words silenced them. "If you cannot learn even the simplest lessons, what use is your life? Go! End this useless existence!"

Budhiya froze. The words hit him like a physical blow. Tears welled in his eyes as he bowed his head, unable to meet anyone's gaze. That evening, he left the ashram quietly, his feet carrying him to the nearby village.

The village, with its narrow dirt paths and clusters of mud-brick houses, was a hub of activity. Women carried pots of water on their heads, balancing them with practiced ease. Farmers returned from the fields, their bullocks ambling beside them, while children played barefoot, their laughter echoing in the warm dusk.

Budhiya, however, noticed none of this. His mind replayed his teacher's harsh words. He wandered aimlessly until he reached the village well, where a group of women were drawing water. The well's stone walls bore the marks of time—smooth in some places, deeply grooved in others.

Leaning against the well, Budhiya stared into the water, contemplating the futility of his existence. As he stood there, his gaze fell on the stone edge of the well. A deep groove had been etched into the stone by the repeated friction of the rope passing over it.

Budhiya's fingers traced the groove, and a thought struck him like lightning. "This stone is harder than my mind," he whispered. "Yet, the rope, through constant rubbing, has carved a deep path into it. If a mere rope can shape stone with persistence, why can't I carve knowledge into my mind?"

The despair that had clouded his heart lifted, replaced by a newfound resolve.

That night, Budhiya returned to the ashram and sought out the Guru. Bowing low, he said, "Guruji, I have been foolish to let my failures defeat me. From now on, I will dedicate myself to my studies with tireless effort. Please guide me."

The Guru studied the boy's face, noticing the determination that now burned in his eyes. "Budhiya," he said gently, "the hardest stone often hides the brightest gem within. Your realization today is the first step toward uncovering it. Persist, and you will achieve what you seek."

From that day forward, Budhiya transformed. He woke before sunrise, practiced his lessons tirelessly, and approached every task with unyielding focus. While others played, he repeated his shlokas. While others slept, he worked through his arithmetic problems. Slowly but surely, the boy who had been ridiculed began to shine.

Years passed, and Budhiya's relentless drive propelled him to greatness. He emerged as the top student in his ashram, earning the respect of his peers and teachers alike. His resilience became a source of inspiration for others, and his story spread far beyond the ashram.

In time, Budhiya became a successful trader, known for his wisdom and integrity. But he never forgot the lesson of the well. He often shared his story, teaching others the importance of persistence and self-belief.

In his later years, Budhiya returned to the valley and established his own ashram, where he taught martial arts and spiritual philosophy. His teachings were based on two simple principles:

1. Continuous Practice: Progress is achieved through steady, consistent effort.

2. Self-Observation: Understanding one's own strengths and weaknesses is the foundation of mastery.

Budhiya's ashram became a beacon of learning, and his legacy endured, a testament to the power of perseverance and the transformative potential of unwavering efforts."

****

The whole class burst out with the sound of clapping. It was as if every child in the classroom had related to Budhiya and then wanted him to succeed.

"Tell me," Mr. Soni continued as soon as the clapping subsided, "how do you all usually study? What's your approach?"

Akash shrugged. "I read the chapter over and over, sir. Sometimes I underline important points, but it doesn't seem to help much."

Rajshree added, "I try to write notes while studying, but even then, I forget things."

"And how many of you try to cram everything the night before the exam?" Mr. Soni asked, raising an eyebrow.

A few hands went up sheepishly, accompanied by nervous laughter.

Mr. Soni smiled, but his tone remained serious. "Let me tell you something: Studying is like planting a garden. You can't just throw water on the plants all at once and expect them to grow. They need regular care—a little water, a little sunlight, every day. Your brain works the same way. It needs time to absorb and retain information."

He walked back to the blackboard and picked up a piece of chalk. In bold letters, he wrote: Practice and Consistency.

"These," he said, turning to face the class, "are the two pillars of effective learning. Let me explain."

The students leaned forward, their attention now fully on their teacher.

"First," Mr. Soni began, "let's talk about practice. How many of you think that reading a chapter is enough to learn it?"

A few hands went up, but most students shook their heads.

"Good," Mr. Soni said. "Because it's not. Reading is only the first step. To truly understand and remember something, you need to engage with it in multiple ways. Write it down, explain it to someone else, make diagrams—whatever helps you process the information. The more ways you interact with the material, the better it will stick in your mind."

Aditya raised his hand. "But sir, even when I write things down, I still forget them after a while."

"That's where consistency comes in," Mr. Soni replied, pointing to the second word on the board. "Studying isn't something you do all at once. It's something you do a little bit every day. This is called 'spaced repetition.' Instead of cramming, you review the material at regular intervals. Each time you revisit it, your brain strengthens its connection to that information."

Rajshree looked skeptical. "But sir, what if we still forget? Doesn't that mean we're not learning properly?"

Mr. Soni smiled. "Not at all, Rajshree. Forgetting is actually a natural part of learning. Each time you forget and then remember, you're reinforcing your memory. Think of it like exercising a muscle. The more you use it, the stronger it gets."

Karni Pratap leaned forward, a thoughtful expression on his face. "So, you're saying it's okay to forget as long as we keep trying?"

"Exactly," Mr. Soni said, nodding. "Learning is not about never making mistakes or never forgetting. It's about persistence—about getting back up every time you fall."

The classroom was silent for a moment as the students absorbed his words. Then, Aditya asked, "But sir, how do we start? What should we do differently?"

"Good question," Mr. Soni said, his voice growing more animated. "Let's make a plan. First, break your study material into smaller chunks. Don't try to tackle an entire chapter in one sitting. Focus on one section at a time."

He began writing on the board:

1. Break material into small chunks.

2. Study a little every day.

3. Use multiple methods—writing, drawing, teaching.

4. Review regularly.

"Second," he continued, "be consistent. Set aside a specific time each day for studying. It doesn't have to be long—even 20 to 30 minutes can make a big difference if you do it regularly."

Anjali raised her hand. "Sir, can we do this together? Like, in groups?"

"That's an excellent idea, Anjali," Mr. Soni said, smiling. "Studying in groups can be very helpful, as long as you stay focused. You can quiz each other, discuss difficult concepts, and even teach one another. Teaching is one of the best ways to learn."

The students nodded, their earlier despair replaced with a sense of purpose.

"Now," Mr. Soni said, stepping back from the board, "I want you all to remember one thing: Your marks are not the final word on your abilities. They are just a snapshot—a moment in time. What matters is your willingness to improve, to keep trying, no matter how many times you stumble."

He looked around the room, his gaze resting on each student in turn. "I believe in every one of you. And I promise to help you every step of the way. But you have to promise me one thing in return: that you won't give up on yourselves."

A murmur of agreement swept through the class, and for the first time that day, smiles began to appear.

"Alright," Mr. Soni said, clapping his hands. "Let's start fresh. Together, we'll turn these challenges into stepping stones. And who knows? By the next exam, you might just surprise yourselves."

The students left the classroom that day with a renewed sense of hope and determination, their teacher's words echoing in their minds. The journey ahead would not be easy, but they knew they were not alone

9

KYP – KNOW YOUR PARENTS

Mr. Soni stood at the front of the classroom, flipping through the stack of student papers. He raised an eyebrow, his fingers lightly tapping the desk in front of him. The students sat quietly, waiting for his feedback.

Mr. Soni (sighing): "Let's see… Arvind, 'My father is a lawyer. He works hard and loves me.' Hmm, okay. Neha, 'My father is a doctor and takes care of me.' Interesting. And Mohit…"

He paused, glancing at the back of the room where Mohit sat.

Mr. Soni (raising his voice slightly): "Mohit, what did you write?"

Mohit (quietly): "My dad is a teacher. He's very important."

Mr. Soni (shaking his head): "Important? Yes, but tell me more. What makes your father special? What makes him your father?"

The students glanced at one another, unsure of how to respond.

Mr. Soni (leaning forward): "You see, I want you to think beyond the facts. I want you to tell me a story. Think about the little things—the moments that make your relationship with your father unique. The real stories that go beyond jobs and professions."

The classroom grew silent, the weight of his words sinking in. Mr. Soni could see the hesitation in their eyes. They didn't know where to begin.

Mr. Soni (softly): "Let me give you an example, Alright?"

The students listened intently as Mr. Soni's voice softened, and he began to speak, almost as though he were lost in the memory.

****

It was the middle of my summer vacation, and I was bored of sitting idle in home, so I decided to visit my father's workshop. Until then, I had only heard about it in bits and pieces—how he worked with metal, how the place smelled of melted gold and sharp tools. I had always imagined it to be a mysterious world, one I wasn't quite old enough to enter. But today, that would change.

The workshop was tucked away at the back of our house, its old wooden door creaking as I pushed it open. Inside, the space smelled of warm metal and the distinct tang of polishing compounds. There were workbenches cluttered with tools—files, hammers, pliers, and tiny brushes—each with a purpose I didn't yet understand. Overhead, the lights hung low, casting a soft glow over the dark wood and the dull shine of metal on the tables.

"Papa!" I called, my voice echoing in the quiet room.

My father, bent over a workbench, didn't look up immediately. He was focused, his hands moving skillfully as he shaped a piece of metal. He was wearing his usual apron, sleeves rolled up, and his hair slightly tousled from the heat of the furnace.

"Ah, you've come to see the workshop," he said, finally looking up with a smile. "Come in, come in. What brings you here?"

I hesitated, looking around at the strange tools and the half-finished pieces of jewelry scattered on the benches. "I… I've never really seen you work before, Papa. I want to see how you make the jewelry."

He chuckled softly. "Well, you've picked the right day to come. I'm making rings today."

I moved closer, watching him as he gently hammered a small, flat band of metal into shape. The rhythm of his hammering was steady, almost like a song. The sparks flew occasionally as the metal hit the anvil, and I couldn't help but stare in awe. It was like watching magic unfold.

"How do you do that, Papa?" I asked, unable to hide my curiosity.

He smiled and motioned for me to come closer. "Here, let me show you." He handed me a tiny file. "You see this? It's for smoothing the edges. Jewelry isn't just about making something look pretty; it's about precision. Every angle, every curve, has to be perfect."

I was fascinated. But then, my attention drifted to something else. On one of the shelves, I noticed a ring, gleaming in the light. It wasn't just any ring—it was the ring.

The one I had seen in The Hobbit.

"Papa!" I said, my voice full of excitement. "This is the one! The magical ring from The Hobbit!"

My father raised an eyebrow, intrigued by my enthusiasm. "The Hobbit? Ah, you mean the one from the story with the power to turn invisible?"

"Yes! That's the one!" I grinned, pulling out my phone to quickly Google an image. I showed him the picture. "I want you to make one just like this for me!"

He looked at the picture for a moment, then back at me, his expression softening with amusement. "You've got a good eye for detail, son. But making a ring like this? It's not as simple as it looks."

I felt a wave of excitement and impatience rise inside me. "Please, Papa! I want one just like it. You can do it, right?"

He chuckled, shaking his head fondly. "All right, all right. I'll make it. But tomorrow. For now, come back tomorrow, and I'll show you how we do things around here."

I stood there, my mind racing with possibilities. "Really? You'll make it for me?"

He nodded. "Of course. But you've got to understand something first. Jewelry making isn't just about what you want. It's about how much work goes into it. The details. The patience. And the lessons."

I didn't quite understand what he meant then, but I was too excited to ask more questions. "I'll come back tomorrow, Papa! I promise!"

He smiled and ruffled my hair. "Good. Tomorrow, then.

But now, I've got work to do."

The next morning, I could hardly contain my excitement. I woke up early, eager to see how my father would turn a simple piece of metal into something magical. As I made my way to the workshop, I felt like I was entering another world. The familiar door creaked open again, and the smell of metal and warm wood greeted me.

Papa was already there, working on a piece at his workbench, the rhythmic tapping of his hammer echoing in the quiet workshop. He looked up when he heard me enter and smiled.

"Well, look who's early," he said, setting down his tools. "Come on in, then. Let's get started."

I couldn't stop smiling, my mind buzzing with the thought of what was to come. "So, you'll make it today? The ring?" I asked eagerly.

He raised an eyebrow, amused by my enthusiasm. "Hold on now. You've got to learn a few things first. It's not just about making the ring; it's about understanding how it's made."

I nodded quickly, trying to hide my impatience. I was so ready to get started, but I wasn't going to argue. After all, this was my chance to learn from my father.

Papa motioned toward the workbench. "You've seen me work, right? It's not just hammering metal into shape. There's a lot of careful planning behind it."

I glanced around, taking in the shelves lined with tools, small stones, and pieces of metal. "I know. But I just want to see the magic, Papa. Can't you make it for me today? Like this one?" I pointed to the ring I'd shown him yesterday. My excitement was barely contained.

He chuckled softly, his eyes twinkling. "Patience, son. You'll get there. But first, I need you to understand the basics. And that means you're going to have to help."

I blinked, surprised. "Help? What do you mean?"

Papa smiled and picked up a small tray from the corner of the workbench. "I need someone to clean up today. Sweep the floor, tidy up the tables. I've got a lot to do, and this workshop needs to stay neat."

I stared at him, stunned. "Wait… what? You want me to clean?"

He nodded, not missing a beat. "Yes, I do. You're not going to learn the right way unless you understand that every part of this workshop is important. No job is too small."

I felt my stomach drop a little. Cleaning? That wasn't what I had imagined. I wanted to be in the thick of things, working with metal, just like he was. But he was already busy with his own tasks, so I didn't have much choice.

"Fine," I said reluctantly, but there was no hiding the disappointment in my voice. "I'll clean."

Papa grinned and ruffled my hair. "Good. You'll see—it's all part of the process. You'll learn a lot, trust me."

I grabbed the broom and started sweeping, trying not to feel too resentful. As I worked, I couldn't help but notice the small, shiny particles of metal in the dust—tiny specks of gold and silver that shimmered in the light. I bent down to get a closer look, intrigued by how even the tiniest bits of metal were so shiny.

Papa looked up from his work, noticing my curiosity. "You see those? Those are pieces of gold and silver dust. When we work with the metal, a lot of tiny bits get left behind. Most people would throw that away, but not here."

I glanced up at him, confused. "Why not? It's just dust, right?"

He smiled, walking over to where I stood. "That dust is valuable, son. Every little bit gets collected and refined. At the end of the month, it all gets melted down, and we can recover the metal. Nothing goes to waste."

I looked down at the dustpan, a little awed by the idea that even the smallest particles could be useful. "That's cool," I murmured, carefully placing the dustpan beside his desk.

Papa returned to his work, but I continued sweeping, now with a new sense of purpose. Even something as simple as sweeping had a hidden value, just like the dust. I had never thought of it that way before.

As I finished sweeping the floor, my thoughts were still on the ring. I had hoped today would be the day I'd finally get to see how my father worked his magic, but instead, I found myself with a broom in hand, cleaning the place. My stomach twisted in frustration, and I couldn't help but feel like I had been sidelined.

I glanced over at my father, who was absorbed in his work, his focus so intense that he didn't seem to notice my growing annoyance. "Papa," I said, my voice a little sharper than I intended, "I thought I was going to help with the ring today. Why do I have to clean?"

Papa looked up, sensing the change in my tone. His expression softened. "I know you want to dive right in, son, but cleaning is part of the process. Every part of this place is important. You can't make a beautiful piece of jewelry if you don't understand how everything works together. The workshop needs to stay clean and organized, so you can work properly."

I shifted from foot to foot, not entirely convinced. "But I just want to make the ring! I don't want to clean."

He smiled gently, setting his tools down and walking over to where I stood, broom in hand. "I get it. But you know, even the smallest tasks have their own value. It's not always the big things that matter most. The little things, the things that seem unimportant, are just as crucial."

I felt a knot form in my chest. I wanted to be doing something important, something that felt exciting, not stuck doing menial work. I tried to hide my frustration, but it wasn't easy.

"Besides," Papa added, "in a few hours, I'll be ready to show you how we make the ring. But for now, I need your help. Every piece of this workshop is important. Even the dust has its value, remember?"

His words made me pause. I glanced at the dustpan I had placed by his desk earlier, the small golden particles shining in the light. The thought of throwing that away seemed almost wasteful now, but I still wasn't entirely sure how cleaning would help me learn how to make the ring.

Papa put a hand on my shoulder, sensing my internal struggle. "Trust me, son. If you want to make a beautiful ring, you need to learn how to take care of everything that comes before it. The process, the patience—it all matters."

I sighed, still not entirely happy with the situation but willing to trust him. "Okay, Papa. I'll finish cleaning."

He gave me a warm smile. "Good. And when you're done, we'll work on the ring together. But remember, you don't rush the process. Not in jewelry-making, and not in life."

As I went back to my task, my father returned to his work. I could hear the steady sound of his tools at work, and for the first time that day, I began to pay attention to the rhythm of the place—the way the metal bent and shaped under his steady hand, how every small movement had a purpose.

Even though it wasn't exactly what I had imagined, I realized that there was a lesson in every step of the process—even cleaning the workshop.

As I swept the floor, my frustration slowly began to fade. The rhythmic movement of the broom was strangely calming, and the dust started to look less like an annoyance and more like an essential part of the workshop's ecosystem. My eyes wandered around the room, taking in the various tools, the half-finished projects on the workbenches, and the gleaming pieces of metal scattered here and there.

Papa smiled at me, sensing the shift in my thinking. After a while he pulled out a strip of silver. I watched as he carefully measured it, his fingers precise and confident, knowing exactly what he was doing. My earlier frustration had faded, replaced by a sense of curiosity and anticipation. Today, I would finally get the chance to make the ring myself.

Papa glanced up at me, his expression serious but encouraging. "Now, are you ready to try making the ring?"

I nodded, a little nervous but eager. "Yes, Papa. I'm ready."

He handed me the strip of silver, and it felt cool and smooth in my hands. "First, you need to measure the size," he explained. "We can't just make a ring without knowing the right size. You'll need to take a measurement of your finger, like this."

He held up his own hand and showed me how to measure the circumference of his finger using a flexible piece of wire. I mimicked the movement, wrapping the wire around my own finger, carefully noting where it met.

"Good. Now, you've got your measurement," Papa said, looking over my shoulder as I carefully cut the wire at the point where it met. "Next, you need to shape the silver strip to form the band."

I looked at the strip in my hand, now carefully measured and ready. Papa handed me a pair of pliers, showing me how to gently bend the metal into a circle. "Take your time," he said. "This part requires patience. If you rush, the metal could bend unevenly."

I carefully followed his instructions, bending the metal slowly, feeling its resistance as it shaped into a ring. My hands were a little shaky, but I could see the ring starting to take form.

"You're doing great," Papa encouraged, as he worked on his own project at the same time. "Now, the next part is soldering the ends together. You'll need to heat the metal and melt it just enough so that it fuses."

I watched as he lit a small torch and brought the flame to the metal, He placed a little square piece of solder alloy where the ends met. When he handed me the torch, I hesitated. The flame was small but intense, and I could feel the heat radiating from it.

"Don't be afraid," he said, seeing my hesitation. "Just steady your hand. Soldering is about control."

I took a deep breath, holding the torch carefully, and applied it to the metal. The edges of the silver strip melted and fused together, creating a smooth, seamless band. When I finished, I felt a rush of pride. I had done it!

Papa smiled at me. "Perfect. Now, the next step is shaping the band and smoothing out the edges. You want it to feel comfortable on your finger, smooth to the touch."

I used a file to carefully smooth the surface, listening to the gentle scrape of the metal as I worked. It took longer than I expected, but with each stroke, the silver became smoother and more refined.

After that, I polished the ring, carefully buffing it until it shone. My fingers were sore from holding the file and the torch, but the effort felt worth it. When I looked at the ring, I saw not just a piece of silver, but something I had created with my own hands.

Papa walked over to inspect it. He picked it up, turning it in his hands, examining every angle. "Well done, son," he said, his voice filled with approval. "It's not perfect, but it's your work, and that's what matters."

I beamed with pride. "I did it! I made the ring!"

Papa smiled, ruffling my hair affectionately. "Yes, you did. And now, you can see why it's not just about the end result. It's the process that matters. The work, the patience, the care you put into it."

I felt a swell of happiness and accomplishment. The ring was mine, and it wasn't just a piece of jewelry. It was a reminder of everything I had learned that day. The small tasks, the patience, the attention to detail—it all came together to create something beautiful.

After hours of hard work, the silver ring sat on the table in front of me, gleaming under the workshop lights. It wasn't perfect, but it was mine. I had shaped it with my own hands, followed every step my father had shown me, and now, it was almost complete. There was just one final touch left.

Papa walked over to me, his eyes studying the ring. "It's looking good, but we're not done yet," he said, his voice soft but firm.

I looked at him, confused. "What's left? It looks done to me."

He smiled. "The last part—the engraving. I thought you wanted the Elf runes too."

"Engraving?" I echoed. "But how do we do that?"

Papa motioned to the corner of the workshop, where a small machine sat, humming softly. "We're going to take it to the engraving center tomorrow. It's a computerized machine, but don't worry, I'll show you how it works."

I nodded, still in awe of everything I had already learned. I had spent the whole day shaping the ring, polishing it, and making it my own, and now, it would have a final touch, something even more personal.

We decided to take a break before heading to the engraving center the next morning. Papa made us tea, and we sat in the small sitting area near the back of the workshop. I held the ring in my hands, turning it over and over, still marveling at how it had come together.

"Papa, do you think I could make a gold one next time?"

I asked, a new idea forming in my mind.

He chuckled. "Of course. But remember, it's not about the material—it's about the work you put into it. The time, the care, the attention. For an artist a silver ring made with love and attention will always be worth more than a gold ring that's rushed."

I nodded, considering his words. He was right. It wasn't about the material. It was about the effort that went into making something with your own hands, something that mattered. The silver ring, with all its imperfections and rough edges, felt more valuable to me than any gold ring could.

The next morning, we drove to the engraving center, a small shop on the edge of town. The air was cool, and the streets were quiet as we walked inside. The technician at the desk looked up with a smile. He was one of papa's many friends, whom I already knew, Bhavesh Uncle.

"Uncle, this is the one I made," I said, holding up the ring proudly.

Bhavesh uncle nodded, taking the ring in his hands and inspecting it. "Nice work," he said with a smile. "Now, let's get to the engraving. Tell me what do you want to put there?"

I showed him the picture of the One Ring downloaded from the internet. He programmed the letters in his computer software.

He placed the ring on a small machine, and the computer whirred to life. The engraving process was quick, but it felt like magic to me. As the machine traced delicate lines on the surface of the ring, I could feel the anticipation building in my chest.

When it was done, uncle handed me the ring. The engraving was simple—elven runes, just like the ones in The Hobbit. It was exactly what I had imagined, but even more beautiful than I had thought it would be.

I looked at the ring, my fingers tracing the engraved symbols. "It's perfect," I whispered.

Papa smiled, a soft and proud smile. "It's not just perfect because of the engraving. It's perfect because it's yours. You made it with your own hands."

I looked at him, the truth of his words sinking in. The gold ring I had imagined yesterday was no longer important. This silver ring, the one I had worked on and shaped myself, was far more precious to me.

As we walked out of the engraving center, I held the finished ring in my hand, feeling its cool weight, its smooth surface, and the intricate runes that now adorned it. The ring was more than just a piece of silver and gold. It was a symbol of all the lessons I had learned that day, from sweeping the floor to carefully measuring, shaping, and engraving the metal.

Papa noticed me holding the ring with reverence, a quiet smile playing on his lips. "What's on your mind, son?"

I looked up at him, a sense of realization beginning to settle over me. "Papa, I think I understand now. It's not just the big things that matter. It's all the small things too. The cleaning, the measurements, the little pieces of metal… they all add up to something bigger."

He nodded, his expression thoughtful. "Exactly. Every little task, no matter how small, is important. The work you put into it, the attention to detail, it all adds up. And in the end, it's the little things that make the big things possible."

"I want to tell you another shocking truth, Remember the whole strip of silver out of which we cut your band yesterday?"

"Of course I do." I confirmed.

"It was the metal I recovered from the dust of last six months."

"Wow…" I said with a shocking laughter "You are not telling me that we have conjured this magical ring literally out of the dust."

Laughing heartily papa said, "Always remember, when the final product is magical, the magic is what time, effort and dedication you have put into it. Everything matters."

I looked down at the ring again, turning it over in my fingers with smile. "Even the dust."

Papa smiled warmly. "Yes, even the dust. Nothing goes to waste. Everything has its purpose, its value. It's all part of the process."

We walked back to the workshop, and as we entered, I felt a deep sense of gratitude for everything I had learned. My father had shown me not just how to make a ring, but how to approach life with patience, care, and an understanding that everything, no matter how small, had its place and purpose.

As the sun began to set, casting a warm golden glow over the workshop, I looked at the silver ring in my hand, now engraved with the runes I had chosen, and realized something. It wasn't just the ring that was valuable to me—it was the day itself, the lessons learned, and the bond I had shared with my father.

I hadn't just learned to make a ring. I had learned that nothing in life is wasted. That every task, every moment, has its value. And that, sometimes, it's the small things that matter the most.

Lessons I learned that day:

Even the dust can be valuable.

No job is too small, not even sweeping.

My father trusted me to learn good values the right way.

The lessons at school were actually useful.

The ring I made was more precious to me than anything my father could have made himself.

****

The students sat in silence, their minds churning. The classroom had shifted. What had started as an ordinary lesson was now something more profound. After a long pause, Aman raised his hand, his voice tentative but eager.

Aman: "Sir… I think I understand now. I have a story."

Mr. Soni (nodding): "Go ahead, Aman."

Aman: "Every Sunday, my mom and I have tea together. It's always the same, but it's… special. We make tea together, and then she plays her old records—classical music mostly. I used to think it was boring, but now, it's like our time. We don't talk much, but it's the best part of my week. No distractions, just the music and the tea."

Mr. Soni (smiling warmly): "That's what I'm talking about. It's not about the big gestures; it's the small, meaningful moments that matter."

Garvit (raising his hand): "Sir, I've got one too."

Mr. Soni: "Of course, Garvit. What's your story?"

Garvit: "I've spent a lot of time with my dad at his shop. I used to just watch him. At first, I didn't understand what he was doing—selling things, talking to customers. But slowly, I started picking up on things. He taught me how to talk to people, how to sell not just products but ideas. It's how he runs his business, and now… it's how I see the world too. I learned more from him than I ever thought I would."

Mr. Soni: "Exactly. Those lessons, even the ones that seem small, shape us more than we realize."

The conversation picked up, each student eager to share their own story. Mohit looked down at his paper, feeling the need to explain more than just a simple "I learned cycling from my father."

Mohit: "Sir, I didn't write this down, but… when my dad taught me to ride a bike, I kept falling. And every time I did, he didn't get frustrated or angry. He just helped me get up and told me, 'You'll get it, just believe in yourself.' I think that's what made me really learn. Not the bike, but the belief."

Mr. Soni (nodding): "That's the key, Mohit. It wasn't just about the cycling. It was about the trust he had in you."

As the bell rang, signaling the end of class, the students sat in deep thought, the stories of their parents echoing in their minds. Mr. Soni watched them, his heart full. They had done more than write creative essays—they had begun to see their parents in a new light.

As the students filed out of the room, Arvind turned to Mr. Soni, his voice full of gratitude.

Arvind: "Sir, thank you. I never really thought about my dad like that before. He's not just a lawyer. He's... a lot more."

Mr. Soni (smiling): "You're welcome, Arvind. Sometimes, it takes a little nudge to help us see what's been in front of us all along."

Mr. Soni sat back in his chair, watching the empty classroom, feeling a quiet satisfaction. The assignment had turned into something more than he expected—he had helped his students look deeper, not just into their work, but into their live

10
THE BABULAL THEORY

The bell rang, marking the end of the mathematics period. The students of Class 8B stretched in their seats, relieved to have a break from numbers. Moments later, Mr. Soni entered the classroom, a stack of papers in one hand and his bag in the other.

"Good morning, everyone!" he greeted warmly, adjusting his glasses.

"Good morning, Sir!" the students chorused, standing up.

"Please sit down," he said, placing his things on the desk. "Before we start today's lesson, I have a question for you all. Be honest with me—how many of you find it difficult to learn new words in English?"

A moment of hesitation followed before hands slowly started to rise. First, Dishant and Shakuntala raised their hands, followed by Akshansh, Navika, and the rest of the class. The room buzzed as students exchanged sheepish smiles.

"It's frustrating, Sir," Akshansh said. "We try to remember the words, but they just slip away!"

"Yes," Anjali added. "Even when we memorize them, we forget them by the next day."

"Hmm," Mr. Soni nodded thoughtfully. "I see. So, you're saying that learning new words feels like trying to catch water with your bare hands?"

"Exactly!" said Ishaan, his voice exasperated.

"Well," Mr. Soni said, a smile tugging at the corners of his lips, "I understand your frustration. When I was your age, I felt the same way. But before we discuss solutions, let me tell you a story. It's about a man named Babulal Patel..."

****

Years ago, when I was just a child, the world seemed to revolve around the rhythm of my family's life—school in the mornings, games in the afternoons, and dinners that brought everyone together. One evening, as the twilight painted the sky in shades of amber and violet, my father came home with a guest.

"This is my old school friend, Babulal Patel," he announced as the man stepped in, removing his sandals by the door.

Babulal Patel was a stout man with a weathered face that glowed with good humor. His neatly combed mustache gave him an air of dignity, while his clothes—a simple kurta and dhoti—spoke of his rural roots. My father explained that Babulal was a sugarcane farmer and owned a factory that produced jaggery and sugar in his village.

At dinner, Babulal regaled us with stories from their childhood. "Your father and I once tried to catch fish with nothing but our hands," he said, his voice hearty and loud. "We fell into the river instead, scaring away the fish but catching a cold!"

We laughed as he animatedly described their escapades—stealing mangoes from the village orchard, racing through sugarcane fields, and outwitting a particularly strict schoolmaster. My siblings and I were utterly charmed. He had the ability to make his stories come alive, painting vivid pictures of village life and their youthful mischief.

"He's such a good person," I whispered to my sister that night as we cleared the plates.

"Yes," she replied, "and his stories are so funny!"

The next morning, Babulal left, but his warmth lingered. For days, I thought about his tales, his laughter, and his connection to my father. But as time passed, his image in my mind began to fade.

Two years later, as life carried on, Babulal Patel visited us again. By then, I had almost completely forgotten about him. When my father introduced him once more, I felt a flicker of recognition.

"Do you remember him?" my father asked.

I hesitated, scanning his face. "I think so…"

Babulal chuckled, his voice just as hearty as I remembered. "Ah, children! They forget so quickly. But don't worry, I've brought something sweet to help you remember me."

From a cloth bag, he pulled out a block of fresh jaggery, wrapped in banana leaves. My mother unwrapped it carefully, and the rich, golden aroma filled the room. When I tasted a small piece, it was a revelation—so sweet, so earthy, and so smooth.

"Wow," I said, licking my fingers. "This is delicious!"

"That's the magic of sugarcane," Babulal said, his face glowing with pride. "It comes straight from my fields. Pure, unadulterated sweetness."

That evening, as we sat on the verandah, he told us about the process of making jaggery—how the sugarcane juice was boiled, stirred, and poured into molds. He spoke of the hard work that went into every block, from sowing the seeds to harvesting the cane.

"It's not just sugar," he said. "It's the taste of the land, the fruit of labor."

As he left the next morning, I felt a twinge of guilt for not remembering him earlier.

The following year, we visited the Tarnetar Fair, a riot of colors, sounds, and smells. The fairground was alive with activity—folk dancers twirled in bright costumes, vendors called out their wares, and the air was filled with the aroma of roasted peanuts and spicy chaats.

As we wandered through the crowd, something caught my eye—a familiar face among the sea of strangers.

"Papa!" I tugged at his arm. "Isn't that your sugarcane farmer friend?"

My father squinted in the direction I was pointing. A broad smile spread across his face. "That's Babulal! Let's go say hello."

We weaved through the crowd to where Babulal stood, examining a stall of colorful bangles. He turned as we approached, and his face lit up.

"Arre! Look who's here!" he exclaimed, his arms outstretched.

I smiled sheepishly. "I recognized you by your face… but I forgot your name."

Babulal threw back his head and laughed, the sound booming over the fairground noise. "At least you remembered my face! That's something!" He leaned closer and added, "For the record, it's Babulal Patel. And don't worry, beta, I'll keep reminding you until you never forget."

He then introduced us to the stallkeepers, many of whom he knew personally. "This fair is a treasure trove," he said. "You can find everything here—jewelry, spices, and even stories."

Before we parted ways, he bought us a round of sugarcane juice, served fresh from a roadside cart. It was sweet and refreshing, and I couldn't help but think of the jaggery he had brought us earlier.

Two years later, during a visit to our ancestral village, I had an idea. "Papa," I said one morning, "can we visit Babulalji? I'd love to see his farm and factory."

My father's face brightened. "That's a wonderful idea! I'm sure he'd be delighted to see us."

When we arrived at Babulal's home, his joy was palpable. "You've made my day!" he exclaimed, ushering us inside with the enthusiasm of a man welcoming his dearest friends.

After serving us chilled sugarcane juice, he took us to his farm. The fields stretched as far as the eye could see, a lush green expanse swaying gently in the breeze.

"This," he said, gesturing to the fields, "is where it all begins. Every stalk is a labor of love."

He handed me a freshly cut stalk. "Go on, bite into it. Taste the sweetness."

The juice burst onto my tongue, fresh and raw.

Next, he led us to his factory, where workers were busy feeding cane into crushers. The air was thick with the aroma of boiling sugarcane juice, and I watched in fascination as the golden liquid was poured into molds to set.

"Do you see, beta?" Babulal said, his voice filled with pride. "This is not just a factory. It's a legacy."

As we left his home that evening, I felt a deep sense of connection. Babulal Patel was no longer just my father's friend; he was a man who had taught me the value of hard work, humility, and the sweetness of life.

Over the years, I've met many people, but few have left an impression as lasting as Babulal Patel. His name, his face, and his stories are now etched in my memory, like the grooves of a well-worn path. And every time I taste jaggery, I am transported back to those meetings, to the fields of sugarcane, and to the warmth of a man who truly embodied the sweetness of life.

****

When Mr. Soni finished narrating the story, the class sat in silence, digesting his words. Then, Dishant raised his hand tentatively.

"Sir, are you saying that learning vocabulary is like meeting Mr. Patel over and over again? We need to keep revisiting the words until we remember them?"

"Exactly, Dishant!" Mr. Soni said, his face lighting up. "The story of Babulal Patel wasn't just about remembering his name. It's a lesson about repetition and familiarity. Let me explain how this applies to learning new words."

He turned to the board and wrote:

1. Keep Revising the Words Multiple Times

2. Try to Understand the Meaning

3. Think About How to Use the Words

4. Actually Use Them When the Opportunity Arises

Pointing to the first step, Mr. Soni began, "Step one is straightforward: don't expect to remember a word after seeing it just once. Repetition is the key. When you come across a new word, write it down. Look at it again the next day, then a week later. Make it a habit to revise regularly."

"But Sir," Navika interrupted, "even when we revise, we sometimes don't understand what the words mean."

"Good point, Navika," Mr. Soni replied. "That's where step two comes in: understanding the meaning. Don't just memorize the word; learn its context. For example, the word 'benevolent' means kind and generous. But if you know that it's often used to describe people or actions, it's easier to remember. Can anyone give me a sentence using 'benevolent'?"

Shakuntala raised her hand eagerly. "Sir, can I say, 'Mr. Soni is a benevolent leader because he helps students in need'?"

"Perfect!" Mr. Soni said with a smile. "That's a great example, Shakuntala."

"Sir," Divyansh asked, "how do we know where to use the words? That's the part I find confusing."

"That's a great question, Divyansh," Mr. Soni said, turning back to the board. "That's step three: think about where you can use the words. Let's take another example—the word 'meticulous.' It means being very careful and precise. Now, can anyone think of a situation where you'd use this word?"

After a moment of thought, Mishthi hesitated before speaking. "Sir, can I say, 'A meticulous artist takes care of every detail in their painting'?"

"Absolutely, Mishthi!" Mr. Soni said. "You've nailed it. When you associate a word with something real, personal, or relatable, it becomes much easier to remember."

The students nodded, their enthusiasm growing.

"Now, the last step," Mr. Soni continued, "is to actually use the words. If you've learned a new word, find opportunities to use it. Slip it into conversations, write it in your essays, or even practice speaking to yourself. The more you use the word, the more it becomes a part of your vocabulary."

To make the lesson practical, Mr. Soni asked the students to open their textbooks and pick a word they didn't understand. The classroom buzzed as pages flipped and pens scribbled.

"I found the word 'serendipity,' Sir!" Nipun exclaimed, raising his hand.

"Good choice, Nipun," Mr. Soni said, writing the word on the board. "Can anyone guess what it means?"

"It's... um... something lucky?" Dhruv ventured.

"Close," Mr. Soni said. "It means a happy accident or a fortunate discovery. For example, finding a friend in an unexpected place can be called serendipity. Can anyone use it in a sentence?"

"I have one, Sir,"Bhavika said. "Can I say, 'It was serendipity when I found my lost diary while cleaning my room'?"

"Perfect example, Bhavika!" Mr. Soni praised her. "Now, everyone write down this word along with its meaning and use it in your own sentence."

As the students worked, Mr. Soni walked around, glancing at their sentences and offering suggestions. The class was filled with focused chatter as students discussed their examples with one another.

As the bell rang to signal the end of the period, Mr. Soni clapped his hands to get the class's attention.

"Before you go, I want you all to remember something important," he said. "Learning vocabulary isn't just about passing exams or scoring marks. It's about expanding your ability to express yourself, to connect with others, and to understand the world better. Each word you learn is like a new tool in your toolbox—useful, versatile, and valuable.

"Think of vocabulary as a journey, not a destination. Revisit the words you learn, understand them deeply, and use them meaningfully. Just like in the story of Babulal Patel, persistence and familiarity will eventually lead to mastery."

The students nodded, many of them smiling as they packed up their bags. The room buzzed with excitement as they left, several of them still discussing the new words they had learned.

"Thank you very much Mr. Soni, It was serendipity, we got you as a mentor to guide us." Chirped Shakuntala when she reached the door.

For Mr. Soni, it was a moment of quiet satisfaction. He hadn't just taught a lesson in English; he had planted seeds of curiosity and resilience in young minds—seeds that would grow into a lifelong love for learning.

11
WATCH YOUR TONE

The classroom buzzed with excitement as the students of Class 9 prepared to celebrate Hindi Day. The desks were adorned with colorful charts displaying famous Hindi proverbs and verses from celebrated poets. The air carried a sense of pride and enthusiasm as the students got ready to deliver their speeches, a task they had been preparing for all week.

Mr. Soni entered the room, a faint smile on his face, as he observed the students flipping through their notes one last time. He was a man of profound love for languages, Hindi in particular, and seeing young minds engage with it always brought him joy.

"Alright, everyone," he said, clapping his hands to quiet the chatter. "Let's begin. Who's up first?"

One by one, the students came forward, delivering speeches that were heartfelt, if not entirely original. Many had borrowed heavily from online articles and videos, quoting famous personalities and offering well-crafted arguments about the beauty and significance of Hindi. While Mr. Soni didn't fully approve of this internet-fed knowledge, he couldn't deny that some of the speeches were well-presented.

But it was Sahaj's turn that truly caught his attention.

Sahaj, a confident boy with an air of curiosity about him, strode to the front of the class. He began his speech with a smile, his voice steady as he spoke about the greatness of Hindi.

"Hindi," he said, "is not just a language; it is the soul of our country. It carries the essence of our culture, our traditions, and our emotions. But today, I want to address a misconception that has been spread far and wide, especially on social media. A belief that English is a rude language."

Mr. Soni's brow furrowed slightly as he listened. Sahaj continued, recounting how many posts and videos online argued that English lacked the respect inherent in Hindi.

"They say that in Hindi, we use words like 'Aap' to show respect, while in English, everyone—whether young or old— is addressed as 'You.' They claim that this makes English a disrespectful language."

The class murmured in agreement, nodding along as Sahaj presented his argument. But Mr. Soni's mind had already begun to drift.

The words stirred a memory, taking him back nearly a decade. He could see the bustling train compartment, the rhythmic clatter of wheels on the tracks, and his old friend Chandu passionately debating the same point. Chandu's voice echoed in his mind, the conviction with which he had declared English a less respectful language.

Sahaj finished his speech to a round of applause, his classmates impressed by his eloquence. Mr. Soni, however, remained silent for a moment, lost in thought.

Finally, he stood, his gentle gaze sweeping across the room. "Sahaj," he said, his voice calm but firm, "you have delivered your speech well, and your points are well-articulated. But there's more to this topic than meets the eye."

The class fell silent, sensing that Mr. Soni had something important to share.

"Even though it is Hindi Day today," he said, "I think I need to share a piece of my past with you all. A conversation I had many years ago—one that taught me a valuable lesson about languages and respect."

The students leaned forward, intrigued, as Mr. Soni began recounting the story of his train journeys and his debates with Chandu.

****

It was a typical Mumbai morning, the air thick with humidity as the local train screeched to a halt at the station. The familiar rush of commuters swarmed the compartment, squeezing into whatever space they could find. I had claimed my usual spot by the window, where the morning breeze offered some solace.

"Arre, Sameer bhai!" Chandu's voice boomed over the din as he hopped onto the train. He was wearing his trademark smile and carrying a small satchel slung over his shoulder. As always, he addressed me with his characteristic politeness, using "Aap" even though we were friends of the same age.

"Good morning, Chandu," I greeted him with a nod, adjusting my bag.

Our usual group quickly formed—a mix of office-goers,

each with their quirks and stories. Chandu, with his respectful demeanor and endless enthusiasm for Hindi, often took the spotlight during our morning chats. Today, however, he seemed particularly animated.

"Sameer bhai," he began, turning to the group. "Do you know what today is?"

I raised an eyebrow. "What?"

"It's Hindi Diwas!" he announced, beaming with pride.

A few heads nodded in acknowledgment, and one of the group members chimed in, "Ah, Hindi Diwas. A day to celebrate our language."

Chandu seized the opportunity, his voice growing more fervent. "Hindi isn't just a language, my friends. It's the greatest language in the world! No other language can match its depth, its culture, its respect."

I smiled but stayed quiet, letting him have his moment.

He continued, "Look at English, for example. They don't even have the concept of respect in their words. They call everyone 'you,' whether it's an elder, a child, or a peer. Where's the respect in that? In Hindi, we have 'Aap,' 'Tum,' and 'Tu,' each tailored to the relationship. That's the beauty of our language!"

The group nodded in agreement, but I felt a niggling discomfort. I admired Chandu's love for Hindi—his passion for his mother tongue was genuine—but his dismissal of another language didn't sit well with me.

I cleared my throat. "Chandu, I agree that Hindi is a beautiful language. It's rich, expressive, and deeply tied to our culture. But I think you're being unfair to English."

Chandu's eyebrows shot up in surprise. "Unfair? How so, Sameer bhai?"

I leaned forward, choosing my words carefully. "All languages are a reflection of the cultures they come from. They're neither superior nor inferior—they're just different. Hindi has its unique strengths, just like every other language. To say one is greater by belittling another is, in my opinion, a limited perspective."

The compartment fell silent for a moment. Chandu looked thoughtful but unconvinced. "But what about the respect issue? How can you say English is respectful when they use the same word for everyone? 'You'—it's so plain, so impersonal!"

I smiled. "That's where you're mistaken. The word 'you' in English is always respectful. Do you know why? Because it uses the helping verb 'are,' which was originally meant for the plural form. Even when addressing one person, English treats them as if they are many—a sign of respect. Unlike Hindi, where we have distinctions like 'Tum' and 'Tu,' which can be casual or even rude, 'you' is consistently polite."

Chandu blinked, caught off guard. "I… never thought of it that way."

"And there's more," I continued. "Just because Hindi has certain features doesn't make it the only worthy language. It's like the fable of Aesop's fox who lost his tail. Remember? The fox tried to convince others to cut their tails because he couldn't bear the ridicule of being the only one without it. Similarly, those who can't embrace multiple languages sometimes try to elevate their own at the expense of others. But being multilingual is a strength, not a burden. Hindi, English, Marathi—they all have their place."

Chandu looked down for a moment, processing my

words. The others in the compartment exchanged glances, nodding in quiet agreement.

Finally, Chandu broke the silence. "Sameer bhai, you have a way of explaining things that makes sense. Perhaps I've been too quick to judge." He smiled, his tone genuine. "Maybe I should start learning English from you."

The compartment erupted in laughter, and I clapped him on the back. "And I'll brush up on my Hindi from you, Chandu. Deal?"

"Deal!" he said, grinning.

As the train rattled toward our destination, I couldn't help but feel a sense of satisfaction. Conversations like these weren't just about defending languages—they were about bridging divides and celebrating the diversity that made us who we were.

****

As Mr. Soni concluded recounting the incident from his past, he paused to observe the students' reactions. Some sat wide-eyed, their expressions a blend of curiosity and newfound understanding. Others looked thoughtful, as if reevaluating long-held assumptions.

It was the kind of change that Mr. Soni loved to see—the flicker of enlightenment in young minds.

Pradeep, a thoughtful boy seated in the front row, raised his hand. "Sir, you said every language is great. But sometimes people say, 'His language is rogue,' or 'Her language is rough.' What does that mean? If languages are great, how can someone's language be rude?"

Mr. Soni smiled, his hands resting lightly on the edges of

the wooden desk. "Good question, Pradeep. When we say someone's language is rude, we don't mean the language itself is at fault. It's about the person—their tone, their way of speaking, their choice of words. A language is a tool, and how you use it reflects your character."

He straightened, his eyes sweeping across the room. "Let me explain this with another story. It's not about Hindi or English this time, but Sanskrit—one of the oldest and most revered languages in the world. You listen, and then you decide for yourself."

The students leaned forward, intrigued.

****

The sun was beginning to set behind the mountains, casting a warm, golden hue across the quiet courtyard of Kalidasa's humble home. The air was thick with the scent of the earth, as though the world itself was preparing for something profound. In his small study, surrounded by ancient texts and manuscripts, the great poet lay frail on his deathbed. His health had deteriorated rapidly, but his mind—sharp as ever—remained clear.

He knew the time was near.

For decades, Kalidasa had dedicated his life to the beauty of language, crafting timeless works that would resonate for generations. But there was one final task left. A piece of work—a creation of immense depth—that he could not complete in his lifetime. He had spent years working on it, but now, in his final days, he realized that he needed someone else to finish it for him.

Kalidasa had already chosen two of his most promising students. He had seen their potential and knew that one of them would be the right person to carry his legacy forward.

But he needed to be sure. It wasn't just about skill; it was about understanding the heart of language, the ability to imbue it with reverence and respect.

He summoned both students to his bedside.

The first, a young man named Aryan, stood tall and confident. His eyes sparkled with ambition. The second, Vishwanath, was quieter, with a contemplative demeanor. His presence was calming, as if the very air around him exhaled wisdom.

"I have a test for you both," Kalidasa said, his voice frail but commanding. "There, beyond the window, you can see the remains of an old tree that has long fallen. I want each of you to describe it in Sanskrit, as I would. The words you choose will tell me who is truly ready to complete my work."

Aryan nodded eagerly, stepping forward first. His voice was bold as he spoke:
"Shushkam Kashtham Tishthatyagre," he said confidently, his words clear and precise. "Dry wood stands in front there."

Kalidasa raised an eyebrow but said nothing. He turned his gaze to Vishwanath, who stood silently, seemingly lost in thought.

Vishwanath finally spoke, his voice soft but steady, as if he were speaking not just to Kalidasa, but to the tree itself.
"Niras Taruvar Vilasati Paratah," he said, a smile playing on his lips. "A spiritless great tree blossoms beyond."

There was a pause. Kalidasa closed his eyes, taking a deep breath, as though savoring the weight of Vishwanath's words.

When he opened his eyes, he looked at both students

with deep affection and pride.

"Both sentences were grammatically accurate, both conveyed the same idea," Mr. Soni said explaining, his voice soft yet resonant. "But there was a difference. While the first student described the tree plainly, the second student chose a more poetic, respectful approach. Even in describing something lifeless, he showed thoughtfulness and reverence."

"Aryan," Kalidasa began his tone gentle but firm, "your words are accurate, and they convey the facts. But they are dry, as dry as the wood you speak of. There is no reverence for the tree, no recognition of the life it once held. Language, my son, is not merely about structure and correctness. It is about how we perceive the world—how we respect it."

He turned to Vishwanath, his eyes softening. "Vishwanath, your words carry a weight that Aryan's do not. You have not simply described the tree; you have acknowledged its spirit, its history. You have shown respect for what it was and what it continues to be in its silent grandeur. This is the heart of poetry, the heart of life itself. You, my child, understand the depth of language."

Aryan's face flushed with embarrassment, but he remained silent, nodding respectfully.

Kalidasa smiled. "Remember, my friends—no language is inherently rude. It is not the words that are harsh, but the hearts of those who wield them. Language is a mirror of the soul, and one can either choose to reflect the world with clarity or with harshness. You, Vishwanath, have shown me that you understand this."

Vishwanath bowed deeply, grateful for the trust Kalidasa had placed in him.

"I will finish your work, Guruji," he said softly, his voice filled with quiet determination. "And I will do so with the respect it deserves."

Kalidasa's eyes gleamed with pride as he nodded. "I know you will, my son. You have understood the true essence of language. You will carry it forward, as it should be."

Then addressing Aryan he said, "And you, my dear child, I believe, would like to achieve prowess in Sanskrit descriptions."

Aryan joined his hands reverently.

With that, Kalidasa closed his eyes, a peaceful smile on his lips. His final task was done, and the future of his work was in capable hands.

****

The classroom was silent, the weight of the words sinking in.

He let the words hang in the air for a moment.

"Do you see now? The greatness of a language lies in how it is used. A person's tone, their intention, their attitude—all these shape the way their words are received. No language is rude, but people can make it seem so by the way they speak."

The students nodded, their earlier skepticism replaced with quiet reflection.

"And that," Mr. Soni concluded, "is why we must not only respect languages but also strive to use them with kindness and humility. The words we choose, the tone we adopt—they define us, not the language itself."

The classroom erupted into soft applause, and Mr. Soni smiled. He knew that this lesson, taught on a day dedicated to Hindi, was something that transcended all languages.

12
STUDENT BECAME TEACHER

Among the regular lectures the festivals kept the balance between studies and entertainment. Children's Day was just around the corner, and the excitement among the 12th standard students was palpable. After weeks of brainstorming, they had come up with a unique idea for the celebration: a storytelling competition among the teachers. The concept was simple yet intriguing—teachers would narrate a story, and a student jury, representing senior grades would score them out of ten. The teacher with the highest total score would be crowned the winner.

The idea spread like wildfire through the school. Most teachers seemed game for it, though a few hesitated. But all eyes turned to Mr. Soni, the 12th-grade class teacher.

In recent months, Mr. Soni had inadvertently developed a reputation as a naturally storyteller. His habit of weaving life lessons into engaging narratives during lectures had left a mark on both students and staff. Everyone expected him to take the competition by storm.

However, when the proposal was officially presented to

him, Mr. Soni politely declined.

"This is a wonderful idea," he said, "but using storytelling to teach or inspire is one thing. Competing with my colleagues feels... shallow. I'd rather cheer you on from the sidelines."

The decision surprised the students. For someone who always encouraged them to step out of their comfort zones, his refusal felt contradictory. Worse, the other teachers began to misinterpret Mr. Soni's decision.

"Oh, so even he thinks this competition is silly," remarked one teacher in the staff room. "If Mr. Soni isn't participating, why should we?"

As murmurs of dissent grew, the mood among the 12th standard students darkened. Their carefully planned celebration seemed doomed.

When Mr. Soni entered the classroom that day, he immediately sensed the tension. His usually cheerful students looked unusually solemn.

"Sana," he asked, addressing the class representative, "what's going on? Why do I feel like I've walked into a courtroom?"

The class murmured uneasily until Sana stood up. She wasn't one to mince words.

"Sir," she began, "I don't know what you thought when you refused to participate, but your decision has discouraged everyone. The teachers don't want to join now, and even we feel like dropping the idea altogether."

Mr. Soni opened his mouth to respond, but Sana wasn't finished.

"You know, Sir," she continued, her voice steady but pointed, "this reminds me of a story."

The class perked up. Even in their frustration, they couldn't resist a good story. Sana began -

****

One day in the morning, Man Singh, the manager of the Indian cricket team, sat in his hotel room flipping through the latest issue of Wisden Cricket Monthly. As his eyes scanned the words of journalist David Frith, his blood began to boil.

"If their pride is not important enough to spur them to wholehearted effort this time, they might as well give way to other would-be participants in 1987," Frith had written.

The article dripped with mockery, stating that unless India adapted to the 60-over one-day format, they had no business being part of the World Cup. To rub salt in the wound, Frith even added, "I would be happy to eat my words if India progressed beyond the league stage."

Man Singh slapped the magazine shut and muttered, "Happy to eat his words, is he? I'll make sure he does, with extra sauce on top."

Just then, Kapil Dev walked in, exuding his usual calm confidence. "What's got you all riled up, Sir?" he asked, noticing the manager's scowl.

Man Singh tossed the magazine onto the table. "This… journalist," he said, his voice heavy with irritation, "has practically declared us unfit for international cricket. He says we should pull out of the next World Cup."

Kapil picked up the magazine, skimming through the

article. His lips curved into a wry smile. "Good. Let him think that. It'll make the victory taste even sweeter when we prove him wrong."

Man Singh blinked, surprised by the young captain's confidence. "You really believe we can do it?"

"Why not?" Kapil replied. "We've got a solid team. All we need is belief and a little madness. We are here to win. Let's show them what we're made of."

India's campaign began with little hope. Fans were skeptical, critics were harsh, and even some of the players carried doubts. The team was considered minnows in a tournament dominated by powerhouses like the West Indies, Australia, and England.

The first match against the West Indies was a shocker. India defeated the reigning champions, raising a few eyebrows. However, a crushing loss to Australia soon brought the team back to reality. The turning point came in the match against Zimbabwe.

India's batting lineup collapsed, and the scoreboard read 17 runs for 5 wickets. The dressing room was silent, the players visibly shaken. Kapil Dev unaware of the fiasco, getting a good bath for himself thinking he still had a lot of time, when he heard the incessant knocks on the door announcing his turn. This he thought was a prank played on him by his team mates. Greatly angered by the thought when he came out, he found utter silence prevailing in the dressing room. He picked up his bat and Muttered "Let's give them something to remember."

Walking onto the pitch, Kapil took charge. What followed was nothing short of a miracle. With an unbeaten 175 runs, he single-handedly pulled India out of despair.

Back in the dressing room after the victory, Kapil looked at his teammates and said, "This is who we are. Never forget it."

On June 25, 1983, India faced the West Indies at Lord's. Batting first, India posted a modest 183 runs. In the dressing room, Man Singh looked worried. "Is it enough?" he asked Kapil.

Kapil grinned. "Enough to win if we believe it is."

The West Indies began their chase confidently, but Kapil's men were relentless. When Viv Richards, the most dangerous batsman, launched a ball into the air, Kapil sprinted backward, eyes locked on the ball.

The entire stadium held its breath. Kapil dived, clutching the ball with precision. The crowd erupted, and the tide of the match shifted.

As the wickets tumbled, Kapil rallied his team. "One ball at a time, boys. Stay sharp."

When the final wicket fell and the West Indies were all out for 140, the team erupted in celebration. They had done it. India was the World Champion.

Back in the hotel room the next day, amid the cheers and laughter, Man Singh held up the Wisden Cricket Monthly. "Kapil," he said, "I think it's time we made good on Mr. Frith's promise."

Kapil laughed. "What are you planning?"

Man Singh smirked. "Oh, just a little payback. A polite one, of course."

The letter was drafted, challenging David Frith to eat his

words. To everyone's astonishment, Frith accepted the challenge. In a gesture of sportsmanship, he dined on his published piece, accompanied by red wine.

For Kapil Dev and his team, the victory was more than a trophy—it was a moment that united a nation and silenced the doubters.

As Kapil said that day, "Belief is what wins games. And we've just shown the world how much belief we have."

India's victory silenced critics and transformed the nation's relationship with cricket. From underdogs to world champions, Kapil Dev and his team proved that belief, resilience, and teamwork could defy the greatest odds. And for one journalist, it was a lesson in humility—served with a side of red wine."

****

Sana ended her story with good note. Mr Soni felt his chest swell with pride, but wanted to ask what was the relevance of this story when she added,

"And you know what?" she concluded, fixing her gaze on Mr. Soni. "Until today, I thought we had our own Kapil Dev in this classroom. But maybe I was wrong."

The class fell silent. All eyes were on Mr. Soni, who sat frozen in his chair. Sana's words hit him harder than he cared to admit.

After a moment, he stood up, cleared his throat, and addressed the class.

"You're right," he said with a small, apologetic smile. "I've always believed in learning from the past, and today, you've taught me a valuable lesson. Leaders shouldn't shy away from challenges, especially when others are looking up to them."

The students exchanged excited whispers as Mr. Soni continued.

"Alright," he announced, "I'm officially participating in the storytelling competition. But," he added with a raised eyebrow, "convincing the other teachers to join, ensuring the management supports this, and selecting a fair jury… that's your responsibility."

For a moment, the class sat in stunned silence. Then, the room erupted in cheers, applause, and a newfound energy that seemed to electrify the very air.

Sana grinned triumphantly, and Mr. Soni couldn't help but chuckle.

"Now," he said, gesturing for the noise to die down, "get to work. If I'm going to do this, it better be worth it."

Sana stood up again, "Guys, but one thing you would have to admit, it was a story worthy of clapps, wasn't it? Where is my round of applause?"

The class cheered for her happily, and why not? She was the hero of that day's story.

And just like that, the storytelling competition was back on track—with Mr. Soni leading the charge.

13
KALUA BAT GO DHISHOOM DHISHOOM

The auditorium was abuzz with excitement and laughter. The 12th standard students had outdone themselves in organizing the event. Bright streamers hung from the ceiling, banners with phrases like "Celebrating the Spirit of Stories" were pinned on the walls, and the stage was adorned with a cheerful Children's Day backdrop. Rows of chairs were packed with students of all ages, and the teachers, the day's contestants, sat nervously in a designated front row.

Devesh and Riya, the lively anchors for the day, stood on stage, dressed to the nines. Devesh, in a sharp blazer, grinned broadly as he spoke into the mic. "Good morning, everyone! And a very happy Children's Day to all of you!"

The audience roared back, their energy electric.

Riya chimed in, "Today is going to be special, not just because it's our day, but because we have something truly unique lined up for you. Ladies and gentlemen, welcome to the first-ever Teachers' Storytelling Competition!"

The applause was thunderous.

Devesh held up his hand dramatically, and the room quieted down. "Now, let me introduce the brave contestants—our teachers! They've been preparing their best stories just for us. And remember, you all get to enjoy and cheer, but the final scores rest with our distinguished jury."

He gestured toward the panel seated on one side of the stage. "Let's give it up for our judges: Daksh, Vishwaraj, Diya, Kajal, and Prachi, our very own stars from the 10th, 11th and 12th standards!"

The jury waved, looking both important and slightly overwhelmed, as the students cheered them on.

Riya took over. "So here's how it works. Each teacher will tell a story, and our jury will score them out of 10. The teacher with the highest score wins. Simple, right? But," she added with a wink, "the real winners are all of us, because who doesn't love a good story?"

The audience clapped again, their enthusiasm contagious.

"And now," Devesh announced, "let's get started with our first storyteller of the day. Please welcome Shivam Sir to the stage!"

Shivam Sir, known for his calm demeanor, adjusted his glasses as he walked up to the mic. His voice was steady, and he immediately commanded attention with his story about Ramanuja, the brilliant mathematician whose struggles and triumphs inspired everyone. His storytelling was deliberate, each word resonating with depth.

Shivam Sir received 38 points in total by the jury members.

Next was Sunder Sir, who brought a lighter touch with a classic Akbar-Birbal tale. His animated expressions and dramatic pauses had the audience chuckling. "And so," he concluded with a flourish, "Birbal once again proved he was the wisest man in the court!" The students clapped enthusiastically.

He acquired the total of huge 42 points.

Anjali Ma'am followed, her energy lighting up the stage as she narrated how Tenalirama had saved the kingdom of Vijayanagar. Her vivid descriptions of the cunning minister's antics made the story come alive, earning her a wave of applause.

Anjali ma'am also bagged the huge total of 45 points.

The stories continued, each teacher bringing something unique to the table—moral fables, historical anecdotes, and even personal experiences. By the time the principal narrated The Tortoise and the Hare with a twist, the audience was fully engaged, cheering after each tale.

But as the event progressed, the students' anticipation for one particular storyteller grew. Whispers and sideways glances filled the room whenever Mr. Soni was mentioned.

Devesh, sensing the audience's impatience, finally announced, "And now, the moment you've all been waiting for. Please welcome the man of the hour—Mr. Soni!"

The students erupted in applause, their excitement at its peak.

Mr. Soni walked onto the stage with a smile that was equal parts charm and mischief. Adjusting the mic, he scanned the room, letting the anticipation build.

"I'm happy to have you all here and to finally have this stage completely to myself," he began, his voice warm and engaging. A ripple of laughter passed through the crowd.

"Some days ago," he continued, "I had an interesting discussion with my 10th standard students. We were talking about parents, grandparents, and the memories they create.

During the conversation, I realized that the current generation is deprived of the simple pleasures of bedtime stories told by grandmothers or parents. As children, we didn't need music, YouTube, or games to help us fall asleep, pass the time, or shield us from boredom. In fact, I believe that depression today is often more about boredom for the current generation. The stories we heard inspired us, taught us valuable lessons, and helped build our character. Our epics are filled with tales of great men, from whom we could learn so much. And even if we didn't always learn from them, we learned imagination. I feel sorry for this generation, so from time to time, I try to share with them what I received from my parents. Today, I'd like to tell you one such story that my mother used to tell me."

The audience collectively leaned forward, the suspense palpable, as Mr. Soni began his tale.

******

This is the story of a boy named Raju. He lived in a small, forgotten village, where the cracked earth told stories of unyielding hardship. The thatched roofs of the huts leaked when it rained, and the dry winds carried dust that settled on everything—clothes, food, and dreams. Life had never been kind to Raju, but it was especially unkind to his mother.

Raju's father had died years ago, leaving his mother to shoulder the burdens of life alone. She worked tirelessly, taking on odd jobs—cleaning grains, fetching water for wealthier households, and laboring in the sun-scorched fields. Her hands were rough with calluses, her back perpetually bent. Yet she never complained, not even when they shared a single roti and watery dal for dinner.

For years, Raju watched her toil, his frustration growing like a storm within him. At fifteen, he was too young to be considered a man in the eyes of the village elders but old enough to feel the weight of his family's struggles. That night, as they sat in their dimly lit hut, a flickering oil lamp casting shadows on the cracked walls, Raju finally spoke up.

"Mother," he began, his voice low and steady, "I've decided. I'm going to leave for the city."

His mother looked up sharply from the shawl she was mending. The needle paused in her hand as her gaze settled on her son. "The city?" she echoed, her voice filled with disbelief. "What nonsense are you talking about, Raju? You're a child."

"I'm not a child anymore," Raju said firmly. "I'm old enough to work. I can't sit here while you wear yourself out every day. It's not fair, Mother."

"Fair?" she said, her voice trembling. "Life isn't fair, Raju. The city is no place for someone like you. It's full of people who'll cheat and harm you. What will you do there? Who will look after you?"

Raju leaned forward, his dark eyes resolute. "I don't need anyone to look after me, Mother. I'll find work. I'll earn money. I'll come back and make things better for us."

His mother shook her head, her fingers gripping the shawl tightly. "Do you think money is so easy to come by? You'll struggle, Raju. You'll starve before you find work. I won't allow it."

"But I'm already watching you starve!" Raju burst out, his

voice breaking with emotion. "Every day, you go hungry so I can eat. You patch up this roof every monsoon. You wear the same torn sari because we can't afford a new one. I can't live like this anymore, Mother. I won't let you live like this."

The silence that followed was heavy, broken only by the soft chirping of crickets outside. Raju's mother lowered her head, her tears falling silently onto the shawl in her lap. She knew he was right, but the thought of him leaving terrified her.

After what felt like an eternity, she spoke, her voice barely above a whisper. "If you're so determined, Raju, I won't stop you. But promise me this: you'll take care of yourself. Promise me you'll come back in one piece."

"I promise, Mother," Raju said, his voice steady. "I'll come back, and when I do, you'll never have to work another day in your life."

Early the next morning, Raju prepared to leave. His mother woke before dawn, her hands moving with practiced efficiency as she rolled out theplas. The soft dough flattened under her fingers, the aroma of spices filling the small hut as she cooked them on the iron griddle.

"These will keep you fed," she said, carefully wrapping the theplas in a clean cloth and placing them in a small tin box. She handed him a bottle of water, her hands lingering on the bottle for a moment before letting go.

Raju slung his bag over his shoulder and bent to touch her feet. "Bless me, Mother. I'll come back with enough money to fix this house and buy you a new sari."

His mother placed her hand on his head, her fingers trembling. "May God protect you, my son. Come back safe."

As Raju stepped out of the house, the first rays of the sun lit up the village. He turned to look back one last time. His mother stood in the doorway, framed by the soft golden light. Her hand was raised in a half-wave, her face a mixture of pride and sorrow.

Raju swallowed the lump in his throat and waved back. "I'll return soon, Mother. I promise."

The road to the city was long and dusty, winding through fields that bore the scars of years without rain. Raju walked steadily, his heart a mixture of determination and uncertainty. His stomach growled, but he ignored it, clutching his bag tightly.

Every step felt like a step closer to a new life, one where he could finally lift the weight of poverty off his mother's shoulders. As the sun climbed higher in the sky, his resolve only grew stronger.

The sun blazed high in the sky by the time Raju's stomach began to protest. He had been walking for hours, the dusty road stretching endlessly ahead, with no sign of a village or resting place. Sweat trickled down his face, and his legs ached, but the thought of his mother's struggle kept him going.

Finally, in the distance, he spotted a cluster of ancient trees shading what appeared to be an old, forgotten well. The stones around the well were mossy and cracked, and wild shrubs grew thickly around it. Birds chirped from the trees above, and the cool shade beckoned him like an oasis in the desert.

"This will do," Raju said to himself, setting down his bag near the well. He untied the tin box his mother had packed, savoring the faint aroma of the theplas wafting out as he opened it.

Inside, there were seven neatly folded theplas, still soft and warm. Raju's face lit up with a smile. "Thank you, Mother," he murmured.

Little did Raju know that this well was not just a forgotten relic of the past—it was home to seven ancient ghosts. They were the seven ferocious bandits when they were alive. They went by the names – First Puri, Second Lal, Third Das, Fourth Maan, Fifth Kaul, Sixth Pandey and Seven Singh. They had lived there for decades, haunting the desolate place, undisturbed by human presence. They rarely ventured out, for no one dared to stop at the well.

Raju picked up the first thepla and, before taking a bite, declared aloud, "Here, I eat the first!"

The ghosts, who had no idea till now that someone had arrived at their well, froze.

"Woaaa, who said that? Is that a human on our well?" asked a ghost.

"Did… did he just say he's eating the first? What did he mean by that? Does he want to eat me?" whispered one ghost, his translucent form trembling.

"It sounded like that," replied another. "But what does it mean?"

As Raju munched on the thepla, he counted again. "Now, I eat the second!"

The ghosts huddled together, their pale faces turning ashen with fear.

"Is he… talking about us?" one of them asked, his voice quivering.

"What if he's a powerful tantrik?" said another. "What if he's so powerful that he can destroy us all?"

"Don't be ridiculous!" hissed an older ghost. "Why would a tantrik sit here in broad daylight trying to eat us? He doesn't look like one!"

"Then why is he counting so loudly?" countered another. "It's as if he wants us to hear him. He's clearly doing this to frighten us!"

Meanwhile, Raju continued, completely unaware of the commotion he was causing. "Here goes the third!" he said with relish, taking another bite.

"That's it!" one ghost wailed. "He's going to eat us all. We are going to be finished!"

"Should we run?"

"Run where? This is our home!"

"Then we have to stop him!"

While they were discussing so, Raju had finished six of his breads and as he reached for the seventh thepla, he counted, "Let me eat all the seven of them."

The ghosts couldn't take it anymore. They erupted from the well, a swirling mass of pale figures, their forms wavering like mist in the sunlight.

Raju dropped the thepla in shock, staring wide-eyed at the seven apparitions now floating before him.

"Stop! Please stop!" one of the ghosts cried, throwing himself at Raju's feet.

"Spare us, great one!" another ghost begged, trembling.

Raju blinked, trying to make sense of what was happening. "Who… who are you?" he stammered.

"We are the spirits of this well," said the oldest ghost, his voice shaking. "We mean no harm. But you… you're too powerful! We know you're trying to bind us with your ritual."

"My ritual?" Raju repeated, confused. He glanced at the half-eaten thepla in his hand. Then, it clicked. They think I'm a tantrik trying to destroy them! He quickly hid the last bread under the folds of the Lunch-cloth.

He suppressed a laugh, realizing their fear. "Yes, that's right," he said, quickly playing along. "I am… a powerful tantrik. I am just about to consume your cosmic energy."

The ghosts shuddered visibly. "No! Please don't! We'll do anything you ask!"

Raju thought for a moment, his mind racing. This was his chance. "Anything, you say?"

"Yes, anything!" they chorused.

"Well," Raju said, trying to sound as commanding as possible, "I don't need much. Just a treasure to help me and my mother escape our poverty. Give me something valuable, and I'll leave you in peace."

The ghosts huddled together, whispering frantically. Finally, they turned back to Raju. "We can give you a goat," one of them said hesitantly.

"A goat?" Raju said, raising an eyebrow. "You think a simple goat will satisfy me?"

"It's no ordinary goat, great one," the oldest ghost said hurriedly. "This goat… produces gold as dung. Feed it, and you'll never want for money again."

Raju pretended to consider. "Very well. Bring me this magical goat."

The ghosts disappeared into the well and returned moments later with a small, plump goat. It had soft white fur and bright eyes that gleamed in the sunlight.

"Baaaaa…" It bleated looking at him.

"This goat is yours, great one," the oldest ghost said, bowing. "Now, please leave us in peace."

Raju nodded solemnly, though inside, he was bursting with excitement. "You've done well. I'll spare you this time. But remember, if you deceive me, I'll return!"

The ghosts wailed and disappeared back into the well, leaving Raju alone with the goat. He looked at the animal and smiled. "Mother won't believe this," he said, scratching the goat's head. "Let's go home, little one."

As the sun dipped lower in the sky, painting the horizon with hues of orange and pink, Raju realized it was too late to reach home. The road ahead grew darker, and he decided it was best to stay somewhere safe for the night. A familiar thought came to him: his uncle's house was just a short distance away.

"My uncle will welcome me," Raju said aloud, his eyes falling on the magical goat trotting alongside him. He adjusted his bag and started toward the small hamlet where his uncle and aunt lived.

By the time Raju reached the house, the sky was a deep

purple, and the stars had begun to twinkle. The house, larger and sturdier than his own, stood at the edge of the village. A warm glow from a lantern spilled out through the cracks in the wooden door.

Raju knocked hesitantly. After a moment, his uncle, a stout man with a bushy mustache, opened the door. His face lit up with surprise.

"Raju! What a pleasant surprise!" he exclaimed.

"Uncle, I was passing by on my way home and thought I'd stay the night," Raju said, trying to sound casual.

"Of course, of course! Come in, boy," his uncle said, pulling him inside.

Raju stepped into the house, and his gaze fell on his aunt, who was stirring something in a large pot over the fire. Her sharp eyes narrowed as they landed on him.

"Unannounced, are we?" she muttered under her breath.

Ignoring her cold demeanor, Raju placed his bag and the goat near the wall. "I've been traveling all day, Aunt. I thought it'd be safer to rest here for the night."

The aunt, a thin woman with a permanent frown etched on her face, gave him a curt nod. Her eyes flickered toward the goat, curiosity gleaming in them. "What's with the goat?"

Raju hesitated, unsure whether he should tell them the truth. But then, remembering how much he trusted his uncle, he said, "This is no ordinary goat. It produces gold as dung."

The room fell silent. The aunt stopped stirring her pot, and the uncle's eyebrows shot up.

"Gold?" the uncle said, his voice filled with disbelief. "Are you serious, Raju?"

Raju nodded earnestly. "Yes, Uncle. It's a magical goat. The ghosts of the old well gave it to me when I confronted them. They feared my power and gave me this treasure as a peace offering."
The uncle exchanged a quick glance with his wife, who was now looking at the goat with newfound interest.

"Well, you've had quite an adventure," the uncle said, forcing a laugh. "Why don't you sit and have dinner? You must be starving."

"Thank you, Uncle," Raju said, smiling.

As they ate, Raju explained everything—the journey, the well, the ghosts, and how he had cleverly tricked them into giving him the magical goat. His uncle listened intently, nodding and smiling at the right moments, but his aunt remained unusually quiet, her sharp eyes never leaving the goat.

Later that night, after Raju had gone to bed in the corner of the room, the uncle and aunt sat by the fire, whispering.

"This boy is a fool," the aunt hissed. "He's sitting on a fortune and doesn't even realize it!"

The uncle stroked his mustache thoughtfully. "That goat could change our lives," he said. "Imagine never having to work another day. We'd be the richest people in the village!"

"But how do we get it?" the aunt asked, her voice low.

"We'll wait until he's asleep," the uncle said. "Then we'll test the goat's magic. If it's true, we'll replace it with one of our own goats. He'll never know."

The aunt's lips curled into a sly smile. "Brilliant."

While Raju slept soundly, dreaming of the life he would build for his mother, the uncle and aunt crept into the corner where the goat was tied. They fed it a handful of grass and waited. Within moments, the goat gave its golden dung, shining faintly in the firelight.

"It's true!" the aunt whispered excitedly.

Without wasting a second, the uncle fetched an identical goat from their herd and tied it in place of the magical one. They carried the real goat out to the back of the house and hid it in a locked shed.

By the time morning came, Raju woke to the sound of birds chirping and the smell of freshly cooked parathas. He stretched and smiled, grateful for the hospitality.

"Good morning, Uncle! Aunt!" he said, sitting up.

"Good morning, Raju," his uncle replied, grinning. "Your goat is ready and waiting for you outside."

Raju quickly gathered his things, tied the goat to a rope, and prepared to leave. "Thank you for letting me stay. I'll come back to visit soon."

"Of course, Raju," the uncle said, his smile wide and insincere.

As Raju walked away, tugging the goat along, the aunt muttered under her breath, "He'll figure it out soon enough."

Later that afternoon, when Raju reached home, he was eager to show his mother the goat's magic.

"Mother!" he called out, running into their small hut.

His mother, surprised to see him back so soon, came out wiping her hands on her sari. "Raju, you're back already? What is this?" she asked, pointing at the goat.

"This, Mother, is our answer to all our problems!" Raju said proudly. "This goat gives gold as dung. Watch!"

He quickly fetched some grass and fed it to the goat, anticipation bubbling inside him. But instead of gold, the goat gave a pile of ordinary, stinky dung.

His mother's face turned red with anger. "Raju! Have you lost your mind? This is your big treasure? A goat that gives us filth?"

"No, Mother, wait!" Raju said, panicking. "It's supposed to give gold!"

But no matter how much he tried, the goat did nothing extraordinary. His mother shook her head, muttering about how he had been fooled.

Raju's heart sank as realization dawned upon him. He clenched his fists and muttered, "The ghosts have cheated me!"

Furious, he turned to his mother. "Mother, I need seven more theplas. I'm going back to the well."

His mother sighed, confused but trusting him, and began rolling out the dough once more.

Raju stormed through the forest, his bare feet kicking up the dry leaves that scattered the path. The failure of the goat weighed heavily on him, and anger simmered in his chest. He clenched his fists tightly around the cloth bundle holding his mother's fresh theplas.

"The ghosts cheated me," he muttered to himself. "I trusted them, and they gave me a useless goat! I'll make sure they pay for this."

When he finally reached the well, it was the harsh sunny afternoon. The air felt heavy, almost charged with the memory of the ghosts' earlier fear. Raju sat down beside the well, unwrapping his theplas with a determined expression.

"Let's see if you'll come out this time," he muttered, taking out the first thepla.

He raised it to his mouth, his voice echoing as he announced, "Here I eat the first!"

His roar reverberated through the silent forest.

Far below, the ghosts stirred once again.

"Do you hear that?" one of them whispered, his translucent form flickering in alarm.

"It's him!" another ghost cried. "He's back! And he's threatening us again!"

The lead ghost floated to the edge of the group, peering up through the dark well. "He's performing the ritual! The same one where he devours seven spirits!"

The ghosts huddled together, trembling.

"We barely survived last time," one whimpered.

"Silence!" barked the lead ghost. "We must act quickly before he completes the ritual and unleashes his wrath upon us!"

Meanwhile, Raju continued pretending, his voice growing

louder each time.

"Here I eat the second!" he declared, taking a big bite.

The ghosts' panic grew.
"We have to stop him!" one of them cried.

As Raju announced, "Here I eat the fifth!" the ghosts could bear it no longer. They shot out of the well like streaks of pale blue light, their wails cutting through the air.

"Stop! Please stop!" the lead ghost cried, falling to his knees before Raju.

Raju stopped mid-bite, looking down at the cowering ghosts. His face was stern, though inside, he couldn't help but feel a twinge of satisfaction.

"So, you've come out," he said, his tone steady but filled with authority.

"Great Tantrik!" one of the ghosts wailed. "We beg you to spare us! Do not complete your ritual!"

Raju wiped his hands on his dhoti, standing up to his full height. "You think you can trick me? You gave me a goat that was supposed to produce gold dung, but all it gave me was filth! Do you think I wouldn't notice?"

The ghosts looked at one another in confusion and shock. "What?" the lead ghost stammered. "But that's impossible! The goat we gave you was enchanted—it cannot fail!"

"Well, it did!" Raju snapped, his voice echoing through the forest. "Because of your trickery, I was humiliated in front of my mother. She thinks I'm a fool now!"

The ghosts floated closer, their faces filled with worry. "O mighty one, we would never dare to deceive you," the lead ghost said earnestly. "The goat must have been tampered with. There is no other explanation."

Raju narrowed his eyes, his anger simmering. "You're trying to shift the blame? I should just finish this ritual right now!"

"No! Please!" the ghosts cried, trembling. "We will give you another treasure. One that cannot fail."

The lead ghost gestured to his companions, who quickly disappeared back into the well. After a few tense moments, they returned, carrying an ornate copper pot. Its surface was engraved with intricate patterns that glowed faintly in the moonlight.

"This," the lead ghost said, placing the pot before Raju, "is the Magical Cooker. It will produce any dish you desire without needing ingredients. Simply command it, and it will obey."

Raju's anger gave way to curiosity as he inspected the pot. "Any dish?" he asked, his tone skeptical.

"Yes," the ghost confirmed. "But it is a powerful item. You must use it wisely."

Raju's stomach grumbled, reminding him of his hunger. He decided to test the cooker. Placing it on a flat stone, he cleared his throat and said, "Magical Cooker, give me motichoor ke laddoo."

A faint hum filled the air, and the lid of the cooker began to tremble. Moments later, it popped open, and the rich aroma of freshly made motichoor laddoos wafted out. Raju's eyes widened as he pulled one out and took a bite. It was warm, sweet, and perfect.

"It works!" he exclaimed, grinning from ear to ear.

The ghosts watched him nervously. "Do you believe us now, O great one?"

Raju nodded, his anger fading. "You've redeemed yourselves. But I warn you—if this fails, I'll be back."

The ghosts bowed low. "You have our word, mighty one."

Raju wrapped the cooker carefully in a cloth, thanked the ghosts, and began his journey back through the forest. He couldn't wait to show his mother this magical treasure. But as the night deepened and the forest grew darker, he realized it would be too late to reach home.

He sighed, looking up at the familiar path ahead. "I'll stop at Uncle's house again," he muttered. "This time, they'll see something truly magical."

As Raju made his way back through the winding path of the forest, the chill of the evening air seemed to seep deeper into his bones. His thoughts buzzed with excitement—this time, the ghosts had delivered. The Magical Cooker would surely prove its worth, and he was eager to show his mother the miracle he had received. But as the evening sun glistened through the thick branches overhead, Raju realized that his journey home would be long, and the hour was growing late.

"I'll stop at Uncle's for the night," he murmured to himself, adjusting the cloth bundle holding the Magical Cooker. "It'll be safer to rest before heading home."

The path to his uncle's house was familiar. It was a modest hut, nestled at the edge of the village, far from the hustle of town life. As he approached the small thatched roof dwelling, a warm light flickered from the cracks in the window. His stomach growled. He was very hungry.

Raju knocked on the wooden door, and within moments, Uncle's cheerful voice called from inside. "Who's there?"

"Uncle, It's me again." Raju called.

The door creaked open, and Uncle's broad, welcoming face appeared in the doorway. "Ah, it's you! So good to see you, nephew. We weren't expecting you tonight, but what a pleasant surprise!"

Raju smiled, feeling the familiar warmth of his uncle's embrace. "I thought I'd rest here for the night. It's getting late, and I have some... interesting news to share."

Uncle's face lit up, his eyes twinkling with curiosity. "Interesting news? Tell me, Raju! You're always up to something exciting, aren't you?"

Raju chuckled and walked inside, where the firelight flickered in the hearth, casting shadows on the walls. "Well, I've come across something quite... magical," he said, lowering his voice for dramatic effect.

Uncle leaned forward, intrigued. "Magical, you say? Now, you have my attention!"

As they settled around the small wooden table, Aunt appeared from the back room, wiping her hands on her apron. Her eyes darted over Raju quickly, but there was no smile on her face. She always had a distant air about her, a sharpness in her gaze that seemed to notice everything. Still, she greeted him with a curt nod.

"Raju's here, is he?" she said, her voice flat, not showing

the same warmth as Uncle's. "What brings you by so late?"

Raju, undeterred by her cool demeanor, smiled at her. "Just staying the night, Aunt. I'll be off in the morning, but I've brought something special to show you both."
Aunt raised an eyebrow, clearly curious despite herself. "Something special, huh? I'm sure you have a good reason for popping by so unexpectedly."

Raju's excitement grew as he unwrapped the cloth holding the Magical Cooker. "This, Aunt, is something I received from some very... unusual sources."

Uncle leaned over the table, eyes widening in amazement. "What is this? It looks like an ancient pot!"

"It's more than just a pot," Raju said, his voice filled with pride. "It's a Magical Cooker. It can cook anything you desire—without needing any ingredients. Just command it, and it will obey."

Aunt's eyes flickered with a mix of skepticism and curiosity. "A magical pot? Is this some kind of joke, Raju?"

Raju shook his head, excitement bubbling inside him. "No joke, Aunt. Watch this."

He set the pot down in the center of the table and cleared his throat. "Magical Cooker, give me motichoor ke laddoo!"

The moment he spoke the words, the air around them seemed to hum, and the lid of the pot quivered slightly. A soft light emanated from the cracks, and slowly, the lid lifted, revealing the rich aroma of freshly cooked laddoos wafting out.

Aunt's eyes widened, and Uncle let out a gasp of disbelief. "By the gods, it's true! Laddoos... just like that?"

Raju grinned, lifting a warm laddoo and offering it to them. "Taste for yourself."

Uncle took the laddoo with shaking hands, his face alight with amazement as he bit into it. "This... this is perfect! How is this possible?"

Raju, feeling the thrill of success, leaned back in his chair. "It's magic. No ingredients, no work, just words. I can ask for anything!"

Aunt, however, was not quite as impressed. Her sharp eyes never left the cooker, and her lips pressed into a tight line. She looked at Uncle, then back at Raju. "Hmm. Very clever. But who would believe in such things? A magical pot, indeed."

Raju was undeterred. "I thought you might not believe it at first, Aunt, but you can see for yourself. This isn't a trick."

"Perhaps," Aunt said, her tone still tinged with doubt, "but such things don't come for free, do they? I'd be careful, nephew. Magic always has its price."

Raju chuckled. "You've been reading too many stories, Aunt. This cooker works—no strings attached."

Uncle, on the other hand, was clearly taken by the magic of it all. "What else can it make, Raju? Can you make anything else?"

Raju thought for a moment, then smiled mischievously. "Well, I've only just begun. But let's see... Magical Cooker, give me a feast! A full spread—puri, sabzi, and sweets!"

Before Aunt could protest, the cooker began to glow once more, and within moments, the table was filled with hot puris, fragrant sabzi, and a variety of sweets. The aroma filled the room, making Raju's stomach growl louder.

Uncle stared in awe. "This is beyond belief. You have a treasure, Raju! A real treasure."

Aunt, however, didn't share the same enthusiasm. She crossed her arms, eyeing the pot with growing suspicion. "A treasure, you say? What's the catch?" she murmured, mostly to herself.

As the family dug into the meal, Aunt's eyes narrowed, her mind working quickly. She had never been one to trust easily, and the allure of magic was too much for her to resist. While Raju and Uncle enjoyed the feast, Aunt quietly excused herself and slipped into the back room.

In the quiet of the night, she examined the cooker, her fingers tracing the intricate patterns on the pot's surface. She could feel the magic, and though she was impressed, something in her heart urged caution. But greed, as always, got the better of her.

She made up her mind. "If this really works, I'll take it for myself," she thought.

Later, when everyone had settled down to sleep, Aunt crept into the kitchen, replaced the Magical Cooker with a regular pot from their own collection, and hid the enchanted one away in a secret cupboard.

In the morning, as Raju prepared to leave, he was blissfully unaware of the switch. He stretched and yawned, eager to head home with his magical treasure. "Aunt, Uncle, thank you for the hospitality! I'll be off now."

Aunt smiled sweetly, her face a perfect mask of innocence. "Of course, dear. Take care, and remember— magic comes at a price."

Raju packed up the Magical Cooker once more, excited to show his mother the wondrous gift he had. But as he placed the pot on the ground and ordered it to give him something, he noticed the change instantly. Nothing happened. He repeated the command, but the pot remained silent.

Confused, he tried again, but the pot only sat there, lifeless. He felt a knot form in his stomach. The magic was gone.

It was only then that he realized the truth—his aunt and uncle had tricked him. His magical treasure was gone, replaced by an ordinary pot.

Frustrated, Raju muttered to himself, "They'll regret this..."

Raju's heart pounded as he walked through the dense forest once again, his frustration growing with each step. The morning sun had barely begun to rise, casting a faint golden glow over the trees, but the warmth was lost on him. The realization hit him like a bolt of lightning—the aunt and uncle had taken advantage of him. They had switched his Magical Cooker for a simple pot, and now, it was useless.

He clenched his fists, his mind racing. He knew what he had to do.

"No one cheats me and gets away with it," Raju muttered under his breath. "I'll make them pay."

He reached the old well, feeling the familiar heaviness in the air. The ghosts had once again crossed his mind. They were the only ones who could help him now, and he knew he had no other choice.

Sitting down at the edge of the well, Raju unwrapped the cloth containing the pot and placed it carefully beside him.

He took a deep breath, trying to steady himself before he spoke.

"Here I eat the first," he called out loudly, just as he had done before.

The words seemed to echo into the well, sending ripples through the still air. Far below, the ghosts stirred. They had heard this before—the familiar ritual that had been carried out so many times before. They trembled, unsure of what to do, but this time, they didn't rise in fear. This time, they were angry.

Raju didn't notice the change in the air as he continued his chant. "Here I eat the second... and the third..." His voice grew louder with each count, his frustration pouring into the words.

Finally, as he reached the seventh thepla, the ghosts could no longer hold back. They erupted from the well in a swirl of mist and shadows, their wailing forms floating before him, their eyes wide with alarm.

"What do you want, boy?" the lead ghost demanded, his voice shaking with a mixture of fear and annoyance. "Why are you calling us again?"

Raju stood up, his eyes burning with anger. He told them everything, "It was so wrong of me to doubt you. And now I want you to give me something that works – something that will make my enemies pay."

The ghosts exchanged nervous glances. They had underestimated him before, and now they feared what he might do if they refused.

"Please, don't harm us, mighty one!" the lead ghost pleaded. "We gave you what you asked for. We cannot control what others do. But tell us what you need, and we will help."

Raju's eyes narrowed. "I want something that will make my enemies suffer and help me recover my lost goods, something that I don't lose ever."

The ghosts cowered before him, knowing they had no choice. The lead ghost stepped forward, his translucent form shaking. "Very well, we will give you one last gift. Something powerful! A weapon, if you will."

He turned to the others, who quickly returned to the well. Raju watched them in silence, feeling a mix of impatience and anticipation. He was determined this time—there would be no tricks, no mistakes.

When the ghosts returned, they carried a large, worn wooden bat. Its surface was rough and chipped, but it seemed to radiate a strange energy, almost as if it had been used countless times before.

"This is the Kalua Bat," the lead ghost explained, his voice filled with reverence. "When you speak the words, 'Kalua Bat, go dhishoom dhishoom,' the bat will strike down your enemies, no matter where they are. It will deal with them swiftly, without fail. And it will come back to you even if you lose it, you can summon it just by calling it."

Raju's heart leaped. This was the weapon he had been waiting for. His eyes gleamed with satisfaction as he took the bat from the ghost's hands.

"I'll see how it works," he said, his voice cold and determined.

Without another word, he turned and began walking back toward the village. The ghosts remained behind, their worried whispers lingering in the air.

As Raju approached his uncle's house, he felt his pulse quicken. He knew what he had to do.

Uncle and Aunt were sitting on the porch, enjoying the early morning sun. The goat, which had been returned to the yard, bleated softly in the distance. But Raju's gaze was fixed firmly on the house, his mind focused only on the task at hand.

Aunt looked up when she saw him, a sly smile curling on her lips. "Back so soon, Raju? Tell me what novelty have you brought this time?"

Raju stepped forward, his face stern. He held the Kalua Bat in his hands, its dark, worn surface gleaming with an eerie energy. Without saying another word, he raised it high.

Aunt's smile faltered as she stood up, clearly uneasy. "What's this now, Raju? Are you threatening us?"

Raju's eyes narrowed as he spoke the words he had been itching to say. "Kalua Bat, go dhishoom dhishoom!"

In an instant, the bat sprang to life, as though it had a mind of its own. It swung through the air with a loud whoosh and smacked Uncle square on the back, sending him flying off his chair with a comical yelp. "Ooof!" Uncle's legs flailed in the air as he crashed to the ground in a heap, his tea splashing everywhere.

Raju simply kept chanting, "Kalua Bat, go dhishoom dhishoom."

Aunt's eyes widened, and she leaped to her feet, looking both shocked and furious. "What in the name of all things holy do you think you're doing, Raju?!"

But before she could take a step, the bat swung again, this time smacking her right on the backside with a whack! "Ouch! Raju, you little rascal! Stop that this instant!"

Uncle scrambled to his feet, his eyes wild with panic. "What is this madness?! What kind of magic is this, huh? I didn't sign up for this!" He tried to grab the bat, but it was too quick, swooshing around his hands and delivering another well-placed thwack to his knees. "Aaaahhh! My knees! I'll never walk again!"

Aunt, now rubbing her sore behind, scowled at Raju. "You think you can just waltz in here and beat us like this?! We're not some kind of punching bags, you... you... mischief-maker!" She bent down and grabbed a nearby broom, ready to defend herself, but the bat had other plans. It swung up and knocked the broom from her hands with a crack.

"Stop! Stop! My back!" Uncle hollered as the bat thwacked him again, this time on the head, sending his hair flying every which way. "I'm too old for this, Raju! I can't take it anymore!"

Raju stood tall, a grim satisfaction on his face. "I've come for what's mine. The cooker, the goat—it's all mine, and you'll return it now."

His words rang through the air like a command. Without a second thought, Uncle and Aunt quickly grabbed the Magical Cooker and the goat and handed them over to Raju, their hands shaking with fear.

"Take them!" Aunt cried, her voice pleading. "Take them and leave us in peace!"

Raju, trying to suppress his laughter, looked at his poor uncle and aunt, who were now both dodging and scrambling to avoid the Kalua Bat, which was swinging with more enthusiasm than ever. Uncle dove behind the well.

"Good riddance, you two," he muttered with a chuckle, as the bat gave one last satisfied thwack in the air, as if to say, "Mission accomplished."

Raju returned home to his mother, the Magical Cooker and the goat safely in tow. His heart lightened as he stepped through the door, the weight of the past few days lifting off his shoulders.

As his mother saw him, she smiled warmly. "You're back, Raju! What's this you've brought?"

Raju grinned, holding up the Magical Cooker. "A treasure, Mother. A real treasure."

And for the first time in a long while, Raju knew that his journey was complete. The ghosts had kept their promise, and he had learned the true meaning of power—both magical and personal. And with that, he could finally rest.

And with that, Raju returned home, victorious, knowing that sometimes, it's not just magic that wins the day—it's a good laugh and a Kalua Bat."

****

The story ended with tremendous applause and great laughter but at the end of the competition the principal madam won the competition, Mr. Soni ended up on the second place followed by Anjali Ma'am.

It was pretty obvious that some of the students were not happy with the decision of the jury. But Mr. Soni had not expected them to decide otherwise, he was happy to see them using the practical approach in the life.

And he was not in the mood of claiming whatever was his like Raju. After all he could not call upon Kalua Bat in front of everyone now, could he?

The next day, Sana was still fuming and spoke with great frustration. "Sir, I still can't believe the jury made that absurd decision yesterday. I think we chose the wrong group of jurors."

Montu added, "It's just as you always say, sir—power concentrated in the wrong hands leads to trouble."

Mr. Soni replied calmly, "See, children, we shouldn't talk about the jury that way. We must respect the chair. Besides, I believe it was a practical decision to keep people in power happy. So, in my view, it was the perfect outcome."

"How was it a practical approach?" Devesh asked, puzzled.

"There's a line from the movie Gifted," Mr. Soni explained. "'Never get on the bad side of small-minded people with a little authority.' When older people with power feel slighted, they can become sore losers, and it can lead to bad consequences. Sometimes, tending to their ego serves the greater good."

"But sir," Pankaj argued, "your story, the purpose behind it, its message—everything was far superior to anything else presented."

"And your storytelling and narration style were truly praiseworthy," added Daksh. "It felt like you painted a vivid picture in our minds. We could actually see Raju and his actions with the Kalua Bat."

"It's okay, students," Mr. Soni sighed. "It wasn't a competition of great importance anyway. Your appreciation is my real reward. Honestly, I kind of expected this outcome—that's why I wasn't keen on participating in the first place."

"Ahh, sir, we're sorry, we sort of pushed you into it, didn't we?" Sana said. "But something good came out of it too. At least we got to witness your excellent oratory performance and learned something important, too."

"And what is that?" Mr. Soni asked, intrigued.

"Never to question Mr. Soni's judgment again," Sana replied with a chuckle.

Mr. Soni laughed heartily. "Come now, it's high time we started the next chapter. Everyone, take out your English Literature textbooks."

14
HELPING ENEMY OR SCOLDING FRIEND?

During the 10th standard preliminary exams, the classroom was tense with the pressure of upcoming board exams.

Rajveer, a quiet but diligent student, had always been serious about his studies. However, that day, he found himself in an unfortunate situation. In the middle of the exam, Mr. Soni noticed something unusual. Rajveer was copying answers from Lucky's paper. It was clear that Lucky was helping him by showing his own answers. Mr. Soni, who had always encouraged integrity, immediately confiscated both their papers, his expression serious.

The next day, as the students sat down for the lesson, the atmosphere was still thick with tension. Mr. Soni entered the classroom and gave a pointed look at Lucky, who was nervously sitting in his seat. Without delay, Mr. Soni began addressing the entire class.

"Yesterday, I caught two of you cheating in the exam," he began, his voice calm but firm. "Lucky, you were caught helping Rajveer. I want to know why."

Lucky looked around at his classmates, feeling embarrassed. He shifted uncomfortably in his seat before responding, "Sir, I was just helping my friend. Rajveer was struggling, and I didn't want him to fail."

Mr. Soni listened patiently, then shook his head. "Helping a friend is a noble thing, Lucky. But there's a right way to do it, and that was not it."

Lucky blinked, confused. "But I just wanted to help him pass, sir."

Mr. Soni nodded thoughtfully. "I understand that, but you see, when you help someone cheat, you're not truly helping them. You're making them weak and dependent. You're not teaching them anything."

He walked to the front of the class and leaned on his desk, looking out at his students. "If you want to help your friend, help them in the right way. Help them understand the lesson in class, help them with the concepts, but never help them during an exam. The exam is not about getting the answer right by any means; it's about showing what you've learned on your own."

The class was quiet, absorbing his words. Mr. Soni could tell the message was sinking in, but he wanted to explain further.

"Let me tell you a story," he began.

****

In the ancient kingdom of Veerdhara, prosperity flowed like the great Narmada river that bordered its lands. The air was fragrant with the scent of blooming jasmine, and the streets of the capital bustled with merchants selling silks, spices, and gold ornaments. The palace, perched atop a hill, gleamed in the sunlight, its walls carved with tales of warriors and gods.

Inside the palace, the court buzzed with activity. Ministers debated trade policies, scholars recited scriptures, and servants hurried with trays laden with delicacies. At the center of this grand spectacle sat King Veerendra, draped in silken robes embroidered with gold. His crown sparkled with gemstones, yet his expression was one of mild boredom.

Seated on a simple wooden bench near a lattice window was Raghava, the king's only true friend. Unlike the courtiers, Raghava was neither adorned in finery nor burdened by protocol. He was a man of unassuming presence, dressed in plain cotton robes, his hair tied in a simple knot.

He watched the court proceedings with a faint frown before turning to the king.

"Veerendra," he said softly, his voice cutting through the noise, "you are surrounded by a sea of people, yet you live as though in chains. You rely on others for every little thing."

Veerendra raised an eyebrow, a smirk tugging at his lips. "Chains, you say? I think you mistake this for a jail, Raghava. Look around. My ministers ensure the kingdom prospers, my generals protect its borders, and my servants ensure my every need is met. What more could I ask for?"

Raghava leaned forward, his tone turning sharper. "You ask for ease, but at what cost? You command a thousand warriors, yet you cannot wield a sword yourself. You ride a fine steed, yet you cannot mount it without help. Even in a game of chess, you have someone whispering moves into your ear!"

At this, the courtiers exchanged amused glances, and one of the ministers whispered to another, "Raghava is at it again with his nonsense."

The king chuckled, leaning back on his throne. "You have a strange way of showing friendship, Raghava. Do you expect me to abandon my courtly duties and spend my days climbing trees and lighting fires?"

Raghava's eyes narrowed, his patience wearing thin. "A leader who cannot stand alone is no leader at all, Veerendra. What will you do when no one is around to guide or serve you? You live as though you'll never face adversity."

Despite the king's dismissive attitude, Raghava was not one to give up easily. On days when the court was quieter, he would lure Veerendra out of the palace.

One such day, Raghava managed to sneak the king into the palace gardens, far from the prying eyes of ministers and servants. The two stood beneath a towering banyan tree, its roots coiled like ancient serpents.

"Now," Raghava said, handing Veerendra a bow, "let us see if the king of Veerdhara can hunt without his royal archers."

Veerendra took the bow reluctantly, the polished wood feeling foreign in his hands. "You expect me to hit a target with this? My hunters handle this for me."

"And what if your hunters aren't there?" Raghava countered. He picked up a clay pot and placed it on a nearby rock. "Aim for that."

The king pulled the string back awkwardly and released the arrow. It sailed past the pot, landing with a dull thud in the bushes.

Raghava sighed. "You're not even holding it correctly. Here, let me show you." He stepped behind the king, adjusting his grip on the bow and the angle of his aim.

"Focus, Veerendra. The bow does not respect rank; it respects skill."

After several attempts, the king managed to hit the edge of the pot. He beamed, but Raghava's face remained serious.

"Now do it without my help," Raghava said, stepping back.

The king frowned. "Enough of this! I am a ruler, not a commoner. Why should I dirty my hands with these tasks?"

"Because," Raghava said, his voice steady, "power is fleeting. What remains is your ability to endure and adapt. If you cannot do that, your crown is just a hollow ornament."

The king laughed dismissively and tossed the bow aside. "You are persistent, Raghava, but you forget who I am. I rule this kingdom, and I have no need for your lessons in humility."

The days passed, and Raghava's persistence only grew. He taught Veerendra to tie knots, start fires, and even climb trees. Each lesson was met with resistance, yet Raghava remained patient.

One evening, Veerendra finally snapped. They were at the riverbank, and Raghava was showing the king how to fish with a simple net. Veerendra, drenched in sweat and frustration, threw the net aside.

"That's enough, Raghava!" he roared. "I have indulged your whims for too long. You forget your place!"

Raghava stood still, his face calm but his eyes reflecting a deep hurt.

"Guards!" Veerendra bellowed. "Take him to the lockup!

Let him reflect on his insolence."

The guards hesitated, unsure if the king was serious. When he glared at them, they stepped forward to escort Raghava away.

As they led him off, Raghava turned and spoke softly, his voice carrying an eerie certainty. "One day, Veerendra, you will wish you had listened to me. When that day comes, I hope you remember my words."

Veerendra looked away, unwilling to meet his friend's gaze.

The hunting grounds of Veerdhara were legendary—a dense forest where sunlight filtered through towering sal trees, and deer roamed freely in the underbrush. Veerendra, determined to distract himself from Raghava's words, had planned an extravagant hunt.

The royal entourage moved like a procession. Veerendra rode a majestic Marwari horse, its golden mane glinting in the sunlight, while his hunters walked ahead, armed with bows and spears. Servants carried provisions, and even a royal chef was present to prepare a feast in the forest.

As they delved deeper into the jungle, the king spotted a herd of deer grazing near a stream. He raised his hand, signaling the hunters to advance.

"Majestic creatures, are they not?" he remarked to his chief minister, who rode beside him.

"Indeed, Your Majesty," the minister replied, though it was clear the words were meant to flatter.

The hunters moved swiftly, their arrows ready. The deer scattered, and the king's heart quickened with excitement.

"Did you see that one with the white streak on its back?" Veerendra asked. "I want it caught!"

The hunters nodded and chased after the deer, disappearing into the thickets. Veerendra, satisfied, leaned back on his saddle, content to let others do the work.

As the afternoon waned, the sky began to change. Clouds rolled in, dark and heavy, swallowing the sunlight. A chill wind rustled the leaves, and the calls of birds grew frantic.

"Looks like a storm is coming," one of the servants murmured, glancing nervously at the sky.

Veerendra dismissed the concern with a wave of his hand. "We've weathered storms before. Focus on the hunt!"

But the storm was unlike any they had seen. Thunder cracked, echoing through the forest, and rain began to pour in torrents. The dense canopy provided little shelter as the wind howled, scattering the entourage. Horses neighed in panic, and the hunters shouted to one another, their voices lost in the cacophony.

Veerendra's horse, startled by a sudden flash of lightning, reared up and bolted.

"Majesty!" the minister called, but his voice was quickly drowned by the storm.

Clinging desperately to the reins, Veerendra tried to steady the horse, but it galloped wildly, deeper into the forest. The king's heart pounded as the trees blurred around

When the horse finally slowed, Veerendra found himself in a part of the forest he did not recognize. The storm raged on, and he was drenched to the bone. He dismounted carefully, his legs trembling from the ride.

"Hello?" he called out, but there was no response. The only sounds were the patter of rain and the distant rumble of thunder.

Veerendra led the horse through the forest, hoping to find his men. The rain made the ground slippery, and the dense foliage obscured his path. Hours passed, and the storm showed no sign of abating.

Finally, he stumbled upon a cave nestled in the roots of an ancient tree. Reluctantly, he led the horse inside and collapsed onto the cold, damp ground.

The night was long and unforgiving. Veerendra shivered in his soaked robes, his stomach growling with hunger. Memories of Raghava's lessons surfaced, unbidden. He recalled the fire they had once lit together by rubbing stones, the fish they had caught with nothing but a simple net.

"How foolish I was," he muttered to himself, his voice bitter with regret.

When dawn broke, the storm had passed, leaving the forest soaked and glistening under a pale sun. Veerendra stepped out of the cave, his body aching from the cold. Hunger gnawed at him, and he decided to hunt for food.

He reached for his bow, which he had carried on the hunt, but his hands trembled as he tried to string it. After several failed attempts, he threw it aside in frustration.

He then looked up at a tree laden with ripe fruits, their golden skins glistening with dew. Relief washed over him as he approached, but he hesitated. Raghava's voice echoed in his mind: "Not all that glitters is safe to eat."

Veerendra plucked a fruit and sniffed it cautiously. He had no idea if it was edible, and the thought of poisoning himself made him retreat in defeat.

"Useless," he whispered, clenching his fists. "I am a king, yet I cannot even feed myself."

Desperation drove him to his horse. He decided to ride and search for his men, but as he reached for the saddle, a sobering realization struck him—he didn't know how to mount without help. His pride crumbled.

Left with no other option, Veerendra began walking. The forest seemed endless, its paths winding and deceptive. Hours passed, and his strength waned. Just as he was about to collapse, he heard a distant, familiar sound—the neighing of a horse.

It was his own horse that had wandered off, only to catch the scent of the search party that had been combing the forest for two days. Veerendra's men, led by his chief minister, spotted him soon after and rushed to his aid.

"Your Majesty!" the minister exclaimed, dismounting to help the king. "We feared the worst!"

Veerendra, exhausted and humbled, allowed himself to be lifted onto a horse. The ride back to the palace was silent, the king lost in thought.

When they reached the gates, Veerendra dismounted unsteadily and turned to his chief minister. "Bring me to Raghava," he said quietly "at once."

The palace courtyard was unusually quiet when Veerendra arrived, his robes still damp and his face pale from the ordeal. He walked straight to the lockup, dismissing the guards who tried to accompany him. The sound of his footsteps echoed against the stone walls.

When he reached Raghava's cell, he paused. Raghava sat cross-legged on the floor, his back straight and his eyes closed in meditation. He looked calm, as if the days in confinement had not touched his spirit.

"Raghava," Veerendra called softly.

Raghava opened his eyes and turned toward the king. A flicker of surprise crossed his face, but it quickly faded into calm recognition. "Veerendra," he said simply.

For a moment, the king could not speak. His throat tightened as he looked at the man who had been his steadfast companion. Finally, he said, "Open the cell."

The guards hurried to unlock the door, and Veerendra stepped inside. He knelt before Raghava, lowering his head. "I was wrong, my friend. I let my pride blind me to your wisdom. Can you forgive me?"

Raghava's eyes softened, and he placed a hand on the king's shoulder. "You are my friend, Veerendra. There is nothing to forgive. What happened in the forest?"

Veerendra took a deep breath and recounted his harrowing experience—his helplessness during the storm, his inability to hunt or climb, and the crushing realization of his dependence on others.

"You were right," Veerendra said, his voice breaking. "I thought my crown made me invincible, but it is worth nothing if I cannot fend for myself. I mocked your lessons, yet they were the very skills I needed to survive. Will you teach me again?"

Raghava smiled, standing up and helping the king to his feet. "Of course, Veerendra. But you must understand— learning is not about a single moment of survival. It is about embracing life itself."

The next morning, Veerendra joined Raghava in the palace gardens. Gone were the king's silken robes; he wore simple clothes, his hair tied back like a commoner's. Raghava handed him a bow and arrow.

"Today, we start from the beginning," Raghava said.

The courtiers watched from a distance, whispering among themselves. "What is the king doing? Practicing archery like a soldier?" one murmured.

But Veerendra ignored them. Under Raghava's guidance, he learned to string the bow properly, steady his aim, and fire with precision. By the end of the day, he could hit the center of a target, a skill he had never imagined mastering.

"Good," Raghava said, nodding approvingly. "But this is just the start. Tomorrow, we climb trees."

Veerendra groaned playfully, and the two laughed—a sound that had been absent from the palace for too long.

In the weeks that followed, Veerendra's transformation became evident. He learned to light fires, recognize edible plants, and even cook simple meals. His hands, once soft and unblemished, grew calloused from wielding tools and climbing trees.

But the lessons went beyond survival. Raghava taught him the art of listening—truly listening to the voices of his people. Veerendra began visiting villages, speaking to farmers and artisans, understanding their struggles firsthand. He tilled a patch of land in the palace garden, planting rice and wheat to experience the labor of the common man.

The courtiers were initially scandalized, but the people

adored their king even more. Veerendra's humility and wisdom became the foundation of his rule, and the kingdom flourished as never before.

Years later, Veerendra and Raghava sat under the shade of the great banyan tree where their journey had begun. The tree was now a sacred spot, a symbol of growth and resilience.

"Do you remember the first time I brought you here?" Raghava asked, smiling.

"How could I forget?" Veerendra replied, chuckling. "I was so angry that day, thinking you were wasting my time."

"And now?"

Veerendra looked out at the fields beyond the palace walls, where farmers toiled and children played. "Now I know that a king's strength lies not in his crown but in his connection to his people—and his ability to stand alone when the crown falters."

Raghava nodded, his eyes glinting with pride. "You have learned well, my friend."

As the sun set, casting a golden glow over the kingdom, the two friends sat in companionable silence, content in the knowledge that they had shaped each other's lives.

****

Mr. Soni looked directly at Lucky. "What does this story have to do with what happened yesterday? When you help someone cheat, you're doing the work for them. You need to let your friends learn and grow. You need to teach them how to hunt their own 'food' just like Raghava did. By helping them in exams, you're taking away their chance to learn on their own, and you're making them weak."

Lucky sat quietly, finally understanding the lesson Mr. Soni was trying to impart. The whole class, including Rajveer, seemed to reflect on the importance of self-reliance and integrity.

Mr. Soni concluded, "Remember, the best way to help your friends is by helping them learn, not by doing the work for them. It's okay to assist them in class, but when it comes to exams, they must stand on their own feet. That's how they'll grow. That's how you'll truly help them."

The students nodded, clearly understanding the significance of what Mr. Soni had shared. It wasn't just about exams or grades, but about learning the right values and becoming stronger individuals.

15
A NEW PERSPECTIVE

It was a crisp winter afternoon, and the students of Class 10 gathered in their classroom for what would be their last lesson before the much-anticipated board preparation leave. The atmosphere was a mix of excitement and unease. The air buzzed with hushed conversations, anxious whispers, and the occasional burst of nervous laughter.

The sharp clanging of the school bell brought the noise to a halt. Moments later, Mr. Soni walked into the room with his usual calm demeanor. His neatly combed hair, rimmed glasses, and the faint scent of ink on his hands gave away his reputation as a meticulous teacher.

"Good afternoon, Sir," the class chorused, standing in respect.

"Good afternoon, everyone," Mr. Soni replied, setting his bag on the desk. He adjusted his glasses and scanned the room. "You may sit."

The students sat down, but the tension in the room was palpable. Mr. Soni smiled knowingly.

"So," he began, leaning slightly against the desk, "this is

it. Your last class with me before the board preparation leave. How are we feeling?"

The room erupted into a medley of voices.

"Excited, Sir!" shouted Parv from the middle row.

"Worried!" Khushi admitted, biting her lip.

"Stressed!" added Gaurav, throwing up his hands.

Mr. Soni chuckled and raised his hand for silence. "One at a time. Let's hear it. Gaurav, what's bothering you?"

Gaurav hesitated before speaking, his tone reflecting his nervousness. "Sir, the syllabus is… it's just too much. How are we supposed to revise everything in 30 days?"

Several students nodded in agreement.

Parv leaned forward in his seat, his face a mix of frustration and confusion. "Sir, it's not just one subject. We have six! History, Geography, Science, Maths, English, Hindi. And each of them feels endless!"

"Exactly!" piped up Khushi from the front row. "Sir, what if we miss something important? Or worse, forget it during the exam?"

Rohit, sitting in the back, added, "And Sir, some of us aren't even confident about the first term syllabus. How can we manage the rest in just one month?"

The room was abuzz again, with students voicing similar concerns. Mr. Soni listened patiently, his expression calm and reassuring.

Once the voices quieted down, Mr. Soni walked to the

blackboard and picked up a piece of chalk. He wrote two words in large, clear letters: "Perspective" and "Strategy."

He turned back to the class and said, "I hear all of you. The syllabus seems vast, the time feels short, and the pressure is building. But let me ask you this: Are you looking at this as a problem or a challenge?"

"Both!" came a chorus of voices, followed by a ripple of laughter.

"Fair enough," Mr. Soni said, smiling. "But remember this—how you approach a challenge makes all the difference. And for that, I'm going to share a story with you."

The students exchanged curious glances, some leaning forward in their seats.

"A story, Sir?" asked Anshika, raising her eyebrows.

"Yes," Mr. Soni replied. "Because sometimes, the answers to our problems lie in the lessons we draw from the simplest of tales. So, shall we begin?"

The class nodded eagerly, their initial tension beginning to ease as they prepared to listen.

****

In a small, serene village surrounded by lush green fields, Dharmadas, a wise but aging farmer, lived with his three sons—Vikram, Mohan, and Keshav. They were capable workers, but their constant bickering made life in the household difficult.

One morning, after another argument over who should plow the field first, Dharmadas sighed heavily. He summoned them all to the courtyard.

"Sit down, my sons," Dharmadas said, his voice calm yet firm. "I need to speak with you."

The three brothers sat cross-legged on the ground, still casting annoyed glances at one another.

"You are brothers," Dharmadas began, "yet you behave like enemies. Tell me, how will this family survive if you cannot work together?"

Vikram, the eldest, crossed his arms. "Father, it's not my fault. Mohan always tries to take credit for my work."

Mohan retorted, "That's because you barely do anything, Vikram! I'm the one who does the heavy lifting."

Keshav, the youngest, interjected, "And both of you ignore my efforts completely! I handle all the animals, but no one notices."

Dharmadas raised his hand to silence them. "Enough! Your constant fighting will ruin this family. But instead of lecturing you, I will teach you a lesson tomorrow. Each of you must bring me a bundle of sticks from the forest. We will talk then."

The brothers exchanged puzzled looks but agreed.

At sunrise, the three brothers returned, each carrying a neatly tied bundle of sticks. Dharmadas sat on a low stool in the courtyard, waiting for them.

"Place the bundles before me," he instructed.

The brothers obeyed, setting down their bundles. Dharmadas picked up Vikram's bundle and handed it back to him.

"Now, Vikram," he said, "break this bundle in half."

Vikram raised an eyebrow. "Break the whole bundle? Father, that's impossible."

"Try," Dharmadas insisted.

Vikram gripped the bundle tightly, straining with all his might. The sticks creaked but held firm. "I told you, Father. It can't be done!"

Dharmadas handed the bundle to Mohan. "You try."

Mohan smirked. "Watch and learn, Vikram." He wrapped his arms around the bundle and pushed with all his strength. But after a few moments, he, too, gave up.

Finally, Dharmadas turned to Keshav. "Your turn."

Keshav hesitated. "Father, if Vikram and Mohan couldn't do it, how can I?"

"Do not doubt yourself, son. Try."

Keshav attempted to break the bundle, but like his brothers, he failed.

Dharmadas smiled knowingly. "Now untie the bundles."

The brothers untied the ropes, letting the sticks fall loose on the ground.

"Pick up a single stick," Dharmadas said, handing one to each son. "Now break it."

The brothers easily snapped their sticks in half.

"Do you see?" Dharmadas asked. "When the sticks were

bound together, they were unbreakable. But alone, they were weak."

Vikram frowned, rubbing his chin. "Are you saying we are like these sticks?"

"Exactly," Dharmadas replied. "As long as you stay united, no one can harm you. But if you continue to fight and separate, you will be as weak as these broken sticks."

Mohan scratched his head. "But Father, we are so different. Vikram always wants to take charge, and Keshav is too stubborn."

Keshav glared. "And you think you're perfect, Mohan? You never listen to anyone else!"

Dharmadas sighed. "Listen to yourselves. You're arguing again instead of understanding the point. Each of you has your strengths, but those strengths mean nothing if you waste your energy fighting each other."

"But Father," Keshav said, "how can we work together when we disagree on everything?"

Dharmadas smiled. "Disagreement is natural, my son. But unity does not mean you must always agree. It means you respect each other's roles and work toward a common goal. Let me ask you this: What happens if one of you refuses to plow the fields, another refuses to plant the seeds, and the third refuses to tend to the animals?"

"We would have no harvest," Vikram admitted.

"And without a harvest, what would happen to our family?"

Mohan lowered his head. "We would starve."

Dharmadas nodded. "Exactly. You need each other. Vikram, you are the eldest. It is your duty to guide your brothers, not fight them. Mohan, you are strong and capable, but you must learn to listen. And Keshav, you are clever, but you must be patient with your brothers."

The brothers sat in silence, reflecting on their father's words. Finally, Vikram spoke.

"Father, I see now that our fighting only weakens us. I will do my best to lead with fairness."

Mohan added, "And I will work with my brothers instead of against them."

Keshav smiled. "I will try to be more patient. We can achieve more if we work together."

Dharmadas beamed with pride. "That is the spirit, my sons. Remember, unity is your greatest strength. Together, you can overcome any challenge."

From that day on, the brothers worked in harmony, dividing their tasks and supporting one another. Their farm flourished, and their bond grew stronger. The villagers often remarked on their unity, and Dharmadas spent his remaining days in peace, knowing his sons had learned the most important lesson of life.

Unity is strength. A family or community that works together can overcome any obstacle, while division only leads to weakness and failure.

****

As Mr. Soni finished narrating the story of the old man and his three quarrelling sons, the class sat in silence for a moment, soaking in the message.

It was Garvit who finally broke the silence, raising his hand with a confused expression. "Sir, it's a good story and all, but I don't get how it relates to us. It's not like we can give the board exams as a group, right?"

The class chuckled lightly, but their curiosity was evident.

Mr. Soni smiled, his eyes twinkling with a hint of mischief. "Ah, Garvit, you've caught on to the surface meaning of the story, but you've missed the deeper lesson."

Gaurav leaned forward. "Deeper lesson, Sir? Isn't the story just about unity and strength?"

Mr. Soni folded his arms, pacing slowly across the front of the classroom. "Let's change the scenario. Imagine for a moment that the old man wasn't trying to unite his sons to live peacefully. Instead, suppose he had to teach them how to defeat a stronger enemy."

"Defeat an enemy?" asked Khushi, intrigued.

"Yes," Mr. Soni replied, stopping and turning to face the class. "An enemy who was stronger, smarter, and better equipped. Couldn't the old man use the same bundle of sticks to show his sons that the enemy could be defeated by dividing them? Break the enemy into smaller, manageable parts—just like the single stick."

The class murmured among themselves, the metaphor slowly sinking in.

Parv raised his hand. "Sir, are you saying we should break our syllabus like the bundle of sticks?"

Mr. Soni smiled. "Exactly, Parv! The syllabus feels overwhelming because you're looking at it as one massive bundle. But what if you untie it, break it into smaller, manageable parts, and tackle them one by one?"

Anjali, still skeptical, asked, "But Sir, how do we do that? We only have 30 days."

Mr. Soni turned to the blackboard and wrote:

30 Days = 6 Subjects × 5 Days Each

"Look at this," he said, pointing to the equation. "You have six subjects. Dedicate five days to each subject. That's 30 days right there."

Khushi squinted at the board. "Five days for one subject? But Sir, some subjects have so many chapters!"

"Good point," Mr. Soni said. He quickly added:

1 Subject = 20 Chapters (on average)
5 Days = 4 Chapters/Day

"Now let's break it further. If a subject has 20 chapters, and you have five days for it, you only need to study four chapters a day. Can you manage that?"

The class nodded hesitantly, the numbers starting to make sense.

"Let's go even deeper," Mr. Soni continued. "If you spend about two hours on each chapter, you'll study for a total of eight hours a day. That's not bad, right? You'll still have plenty of time to eat, sleep, and even relax."

"But Sir," Anshika interjected, "what if we don't understand a topic or fall behind? Won't that mess up the whole schedule?"

"Good question, Anshika," Mr. Soni said, nodding.

"Here's the thing: schedules are meant to guide you, not stress you. If you don't understand something, spend an extra hour the next day catching up. The key is to stay consistent and not let one setback discourage you."

Aman raised his hand. "Sir, what about subjects like Maths or Science where we need to practice more?"

"Ah, excellent point," Mr. Soni said. "For subjects like Maths, allocate more time to practice problems. You can adjust your schedule based on the difficulty of the subject. For example, if you're faster at revising Hindi, you can borrow extra time for Maths or Science."

Deepika raised her hand hesitantly. "Sir, does this mean that the story of the sticks is not just about unity but also about strategy?"

Mr. Soni's face lit up with a smile. "Exactly, Deepika! The story is about both. Sometimes, unity makes you stronger. Other times, dividing a problem into smaller parts makes it manageable. The wisdom lies in knowing which approach to use."

The class seemed to relax, the overwhelming weight of their syllabus beginning to feel less daunting.

Mr. Soni looked at the clock and realized their time was almost up. "Let me leave you with one last thought," he said, his tone growing serious but encouraging. "Success in these exams isn't just about hard work—it's about smart work. Break your problems into smaller pieces, stay consistent, and most importantly, believe in yourself. You have everything you need to succeed."

The students sat up straighter, their faces a mix of determination and relief. The bell rang, but no one moved immediately, as if they were savoring the moment of clarity

Mr. Soni had given them.

"Thank you, Sir," said Parv, standing up.

"Good luck, everyone," Mr. Soni replied, his voice warm. "Remember the story and make it your own."

16
CARPE DIEM

The hall was buzzing with an unusual mix of excitement and nervousness as the students gathered for their farewell function. The sound of footsteps echoed off the walls as everyone, dressed in their finest clothes, mingled with their friends one last time before the vacation break.

A group of 12th standard students huddled in a corner, their faces drawn with concern. Harsh, Montu, and Devesh were talking in low voices, their words laced with unease.

"I still can't believe it's all over," Montu said, running a hand through his hair. "The exams, the stress—it's done. But now, the results… What if I don't get the marks I need? What if my parents are disappointed?"

Devesh, who had been staring into the distance, turned to face him. "Yeah, that's been bothering me too. I keep thinking about the relatives. You know how they're always so quick to comment—'Oh, so and so did better than you,' or 'What happened, didn't study enough?' I can already hear it in my head."

Harsh, who had been quietly listening to the conversation, let out a long sigh. "I get it. Everyone's got their expectations, and the pressure is unreal. But I don't think we should let it get to us. I mean, the whole world is watching, right? What if I don't meet their expectations?"

"Exactly!" Montu said, his voice rising with frustration. "Everyone expects us to have everything figured out. What career we're going to take, what college we're going to go to, what stream we're going to follow. But it's all so much, and nobody really tells us how to handle it."

The conversation began to spiral, each student voicing a new fear or worry. A few others joined in, some talking about their vacation plans, some lamenting their lack of clear direction after the exams. The chatter was constant, a cacophony of voices all struggling with the same thoughts: What now?

Sanya, one of the 10th standard students, overheard their conversation and joined the group. "You guys seem really worked up," she said, trying to offer some comfort. "I mean, look at us! We're in the same boat—no clue what comes next. No exams to prepare for, no routine to follow. What if we end up making the wrong choice?"

She looked around at the 10th standard group, a mix of blank faces and anxious expressions. "I feel like I'm standing still, like everything is frozen. The future just seems… unclear."

Nikita, another 10th standard student, nodded in agreement. "I get that too. It's like, for the first time, I don't have anything planned. No more subjects to study, no more tests to prepare for. It's like everyone else is moving forward, but I'm stuck, unsure of what to do next."

"I don't even know what I'm supposed to choose for the next year!" Sanya added. "Science? Commerce? Arts? My parents are pushing me toward science because they think I should become a doctor. But I don't know if that's what I want."

A silence fell over the group as the weight of their concerns hung in the air. The conversations around them seemed to fade as their worries consumed them.

"I feel like I don't even know who I am anymore," Nikita said quietly, her voice barely above a whisper. "For so many years, I've been following a script. And now, suddenly, there's no script. There's just… nothing."

Harsh's gaze shifted from his friends to the teacher standing at the back of the room. Mr. Soni had been quietly observing all of them, his face soft with understanding. He was a teacher who never seemed to rush in with answers but preferred to let his students express themselves, giving them the space to work through their own feelings. Today, though, he had an extra layer of empathy in his expression.

As the students discussed in their little groups, murmuring to each other, the weight of their anxieties lingered in the room. Their voices grew quieter as Mr. Soni proceeded to have little chats with them, observing with a serene expression, his hands clasped together in front of him. He was the one person who had been a constant in their lives, always calm, always patient, yet somehow, always knowing exactly when to speak and when to simply listen.

Harsh looked around at his friends. He could see their worry, their frustration—he could feel it in himself, too. The uncertainty, the overwhelming pressure of expectations—it was something they all shared. But there was something else he had been thinking about, something Mr. Soni had said to him two years ago, back when he, too, had stood in their shoes. Harsh had always been drawn to Mr. Soni's quiet wisdom.

He glanced at the teacher again, feeling an unspoken connection between them. Mr. Soni's eyes met his for a brief moment, and in that instant, Harsh understood. This was the time to speak, to share something important.

Harsh stood up, his voice suddenly clear and determined, "Hello my friends, especially the 10th standard students, I want to talk to you all today."

"You know," he began, his voice cutting through the murmurs, "I remember feeling just like you two years ago. I was sitting in this same hall, after the 10th exams, feeling like I was drowning in confusion. I thought I needed to have everything figured out right away. I was so worried about my marks, about what everyone would think—what my parents would say, what the relatives would say. And then, Mr. Soni told us a story that day, a story that helped me make sense of all of it."

The room grew quieter, all eyes turning toward Harsh. His words had a quiet intensity, and his classmates could sense that he wasn't just talking about any ordinary memory. This was something that had deeply impacted him.

He smiled faintly as he caught Mr. Soni's gaze once more. "It was a story about a mouse," Harsh continued "A mouse with seven tails. And today, I want to share it with you all, especially in front of Mr. Soni, who inspired us all with this story."

Mr. Soni's lips curled into a small smile, encouraging Harsh to continue.

"Alright, so here goes," Harsh said, clearing his throat.

****

Once upon a time, in a faraway land, there was a mouse. But

this wasn't just any ordinary mouse—no, this mouse was different. He had seven tails. Not one, not two, but seven! He was so proud of his tails, and he wanted everyone to see them. So, he would go around to all the other animals, showing them off. 'Look at my tails!' he'd say. 'Aren't they amazing?'"

The mouse was very proud of his tails, and he couldn't wait for his first day at school. He imagined all the excitement, all the attention he would receive from his classmates. In his mind, everyone would look at him in awe, admiring his special feature.

But when he reached school, the reality was far different from what he had imagined.

The moment he entered the schoolyard, the other animals looked at him, then began to snicker. "Boo huuu, the mouse got seven tails!" one of the squirrels shouted, pointing and giggling. "Ayyy ooo, the mouse got seven tails!" a rabbit joined in, laughing hysterically.

The mouse's face flushed with embarrassment, and his heart sank. He had hoped for admiration, but instead, he was the subject of ridicule. The other students made fun of him all day long, mimicking the way his tails swayed behind him, making cruel jokes. He felt smaller and smaller as the day went on, and by the time the school bell rang, he was crushed.

When he got home, he couldn't hold back his tears. "Maybe seven tails were too many," he thought to himself. He was tired of being laughed at. So, he decided to do something about it. That evening, he chopped off one of his tails, thinking that perhaps fewer tails would be better.

The next day, with only six tails left, he walked into school with a renewed sense of hope. "This will surely make them stop teasing me," he thought, his heart brimming with confidence.

But the moment he arrived at school, the teasing began again. "Boo huuu, the mouse got six tails!" "Ayyy ooo, the mouse got six tails!" The laughter echoed through the schoolyard.

The mouse's heart sank once more. He went home that evening, feeling defeated, and thought, "Maybe six tails are still too many." So, he chopped off another tail, leaving him with only five.

The next day, he walked into school with five tails, hoping it would be enough. But again, the jeering began. "Boo huuu, the mouse got five tails!" "Ayyy ooo, the mouse got five tails!" The teasing never stopped, no matter how many tails he had.

Each evening, the mouse chopped off another tail, one by one, until he was left with only one tail, just like the others. But even then, the teasing didn't stop. "Boo huuu, the mouse got one tail!" "Ayyy ooo, the mouse got one tail!" The laughter still rang in his ears.

Finally, he thought, "I know what to do. I'll chop off my last tail. Then, there will be nothing left for them to tease me about." So, he cut off his final tail, and for the first time in his life, he had no tail at all.

The next day, he entered the school with no tail, hoping the teasing would finally end. But once again, he heard the familiar voices, the laughter, and the jeering. "Boo huuu, the mouse got no tail!" "Ayyy ooo, the mouse got no tail!"

The mouse stood there, utterly defeated, staring at the ground. He realized, with a heavy heart, that no matter what he did, no matter how much he changed himself, there would always be someone who found a reason to tease him. The world would always have expectations, always have something to say about who he was and how he looked.

He sat down on the grass, feeling the weight of his realization. No matter how hard he tried, he could never satisfy everyone's expectations. And as he sat there, he understood the most important lesson of all—he didn't need to.

It didn't matter how many tails he had, or even if he had none at all. What truly mattered was being true to himself, no matter what the world said.

****

Harsh paused for a moment, letting the weight of the story sink in. His eyes scanned the room, locking with each person's gaze. "And the mouse… he realized something," Harsh continued. "No matter how hard he tried, no matter what he did, the world would never understand him the way he understood himself. The world would always want him to fit in, to follow their rules, their expectations. But even if he did, they would still want more. So, in the end, the mouse learned something important."

Harsh took a deep breath and looked at his classmates. "He learned that it didn't matter if others understood him. It didn't matter if they approved of his seven tails or not. What mattered was that he was true to himself. He didn't need to change for anyone, and neither do we."

Harsh let the silence settle for a moment, allowing his classmates to absorb the message of the story. The room was still. You could almost feel the collective shift in the atmosphere, the tension that had been so present just moments ago now beginning to ease. Harsh could see the gears turning in their minds, each student reflecting on what the mouse's journey had meant for them.

Finally, Harsh spoke again, his voice clear and confident. "So, the mouse learned that no matter how much he tried to please others, he would never be able to meet their expectations. The world will always have opinions about you—what you should do, how you should behave, what choices you should make. And even if you try your best to fit into their mold, even if you follow their rules, they'll always want something more."

He paused, his gaze drifting over his classmates, who were hanging on to every word. "The lesson isn't that you should stop caring about others. It's not about ignoring the people who matter to you—your family, your friends. But it's about realizing that you can't let the world dictate your life. You can't let their expectations box you in."

Harsh stepped forward slightly, his posture relaxed but his words carrying weight. "It's your life, your choices. No one else can make those decisions for you. And honestly, it's okay if you don't have everything figured out. We're not supposed to have all the answers right now. The important thing is that we're true to ourselves and the path we want to follow."

He smiled, feeling a sense of clarity that had eluded him just a moment before. "I know some of you are worried about your results. You're anxious about what your parents or relatives will say. Trust me, I've been there. But we don't need to let those fears control us. We don't need to rush into making decisions about what we're going to do next. We have time."

There was a sense of calm that spread over the room, like a collective sigh of relief. The students were slowly absorbing what Harsh was saying. The pressure they had been feeling— about exams, results, the future—seemed to ease, just a little.

Pankaj, who had been quietly reflecting on Harsh's words, spoke up. "I think you're right, Harsh. All this time, I've been so focused on what everyone expects from me—parents, relatives, even classmates. It's like I've been living my life based on other people's plans for me."

Montu nodded in agreement. "Same here. I've been worried about my results, about my future, and I didn't even stop to think about what I actually want to do."

Harsh gave them a reassuring smile. "Exactly. We get so caught up in other people's expectations that we forget to ask ourselves what we really want. And the truth is, it's okay not to have a clear plan right now. It's okay to be uncertain. What matters is that you're not rushing into decisions just because of pressure. Take your time, and when you're ready, make your choice."

He paused for a moment, letting his words sink in. The room felt lighter now, the tension fading, replaced by a quiet sense of understanding. "As for me," Harsh continued, "I've thought about my options too. But right now, I've decided I'm going to wait for the results to come in before making any big decisions. I'm not going to rush into anything just because I feel like I have to. There's no need for that."

He glanced at Mr. Soni, who was watching him with a quiet pride in his eyes. "I think that's something I learned from Mr. Soni. He always says, 'Carpe Diem.' Enjoy the day, live in the present. And I think that's what I'm going to do."

The room seemed to pause for a moment as everyone took in the words. The phrase, "Carpe Diem," sounded like a simple motto, but in the context of everything they had been discussing, it carried profound weight. It wasn't just about enjoying the present—it was about embracing the now, not letting the pressure of the future steal the joy of today.

Harsh's voice softened as he finished, "So, I'm going to spend this vacation exploring things I've never had time for—hobbies I've been putting off, spending time with family and friends, doing things just for the sake of doing them, No expectations, Just plain simple LIVING."

There was a quiet shift in the room. The tension had completely dissolved, replaced by a sense of calm. Students who had been anxious just moments ago now felt a weight lifted off their shoulders. They didn't need to have it all figured out. They could enjoy the present, breathe, and trust that they had time to figure out their future.

ABOUT THE AUTHOR

Sameer Sagar aka Sammy Sir is an inspiring educator with over a decade of teaching experience, having mentored more than 10,000 students. His passion for shaping young minds and creating a welcoming environment in classrooms has defined his career. Drawing from this rich journey, Sameer has crafted Life Between the Lines, a book set in a fictional school that reflects the challenges, joys, and transformative moments of education.

A storyteller at heart, Sameer dreams of building a fictional world as immersive and timeless as those created by J.R.R. Tolkien and J.K. Rowling. Through his stories, he seeks to spark meaningful change in the world while inspiring readers to dream big and think deeply.

A huge fan of Gabriel Iglesias, Sameer considers him as his teacher who taught him how to actually tell his stories.

You can follow his thought provoking motivational tidbits on his Instagram: @thoughtivator

* 9 7 9 8 8 9 6 9 9 1 6 0 1 *